Apache Trail

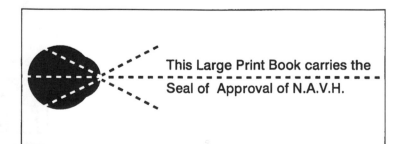

Apache Trail

LAURAN PAINE

G.K. Hall & Co. • Thorndike, Maine

Published in 2000 by arrangement with Golden West Literary Agency

G.K. Hall Large Print Paperback Series.

The text of this Large Print edition is unabridged.
Other aspects of the book may vary from the original edition.

Set in 16 pt. Plantin.

Printed in the United States on permanent paper.

Library of Congress Cataloging-in-Publication Data

Paine, Lauran.
    Apache Trail / by Lauran Paine.
      p. cm.
    ISBN 0-7838-8928-3 (lg. print : sc : alk. paper)
    1. Frontier and pioneer life — Arizona — Fiction. 2. Apache
Indians — Wars — Fiction. 3. Large type books. I. Title.
PS3566.A34 A84 2000
813´.54—dc21
                                               99-054980

Apache Trail

Chapter 1

Karen joined Grady for a moment where he stood in the shade, watching the man with the inscrutable blue eyes get down off his horse. She knew what Grady was thinking because she was thinking the same thing. She probed her mind for words to describe the man who had dismounted and was slapping dull grey dust from his pants.

She had a thorough impression of the rider. He stood wide-shouldered, powerful of arm and lean of flank. He had calm lips sucked back a little, flattened from habit, and he was unsmiling, as though he had forgotten how to smile perhaps, or hadn't done it for so long that now it required an effort.

His face looked as though some dark, brooding knowledge, granite-hard and beyond the reach of other people, had changed him.

Karen knew him as well as did anyone, at Arizona's backwash settlement of Melton, yet in all personal respects he was a mystery. There was indomitable reliance in his expression, and a flood of confidence lay in the depths of his sharp eyes.

He had, Karen thought, a deep and powerful acceptance of everything he had seen and lived through; an acceptance that permitted no questioning or rebellion. Acceptance that had bent him some way, inwardly, with the necessity of living.

The scars of struggle were in his face. He was, she knew, stronger than anything he had journeyed through thus far in life, and he was too strong ever to break.

In short, he was a strange, quiet man with a bitter blue stare in his eyes that had a shade of melancholy, and a body and spirit fitted to the barren land.

He finished tying his horse in the shade and looked over at her — past her — to Grady Stewart. He nodded once and strolled over under the brush-thatched ramada-porch where they stood. His eyes never left Grady's face, but they had an unusual habit of seeming to waver, as though to see on both sides of the thing he was looking at.

"Ma'am," he said without inflection, and bent a little from the middle. Then he looked past her and grunted, "Grady."

Grady stirred. The heat was suffocating even under the ramada. He leaned against the adobe wall and plunged his fisted hands deeper into his pockets.

"Hot, Will. Hotter'n blue blazes."

Grady's remark was as listless as it was futile. No one ever had to remark on summertime Arizona weather. It was always hot. So hot that men went insane from it sometimes, and lizards panted, while rattlers and gila monsters went into a torpid stupor, and even the Indians and Mexicans, insulated with dark, oily pigmentation, suffered.

"Yes," the hard-muscled man said off-handedly, "it's hot. Getting hotter, too."

Karen looked up swiftly at him. There was a double meaning to his soft, drawled words. With rare insight she asked her question: "Indians?"

His blue glance dropped to her. "Apaches, ma'am."

Grady Stewart grunted as though nothing surprised him any more. "Now what, Will?"

"They caught a stage near Florence and some freighters on the desert near Tombstone."

For a moment no one spoke. Grady Stewart's dry eyes moved just a fraction. Karen felt a quick finger of tightening fear claw at her stomach.

Grady let his breath out with a smothered, rasping sound. For a moment he didn't speak, and when he did it showed how his mind worked. "When folks know they're off the reservation, why don't they fort up and wait it out? What's the sense of tempting fate?" Grady looked morosely at Will. "Did you come through from there?"

"Yes, I could smell the smoke still in the air. They burned the stage and killed two horses. Took the others, I reckon."

"How many were killed?" Karen asked.

"I don't know. I'd guess there had been four in the stage. It looked like it might have been two women and two men — from scraps of clothing I found."

"Tortured?" she asked.

He looked at her with annoyance on his face. "No, ma'am, not tortured."

She felt his ire without understanding it and lapsed back into listening silence.

Grady felt more disgust than pity. It showed in his tone. "Well, maybe folks'll stay home now," he said. "We just recover from one brawl and they go out again. How's anyone expect businessmen to keep going with things like this, I'd like to know."

"They don't, Grady. You're supposed to wait it out like everyone else has to."

"How long this time?" Grady asked bitterly.

There was silence after that.

Karen looked straight ahead, out where saffron-blue shadows were circling the distant craggy spires of the mountains. Into the distance where the heat haze danced and jerked and writhed; smoky-looking and curling hot. The smashing rays of a lemon-yellow sun poured great floods of endless fury down, and nothing moved as far as she could see.

All the immensity of Arizona was around her, defiantly brooding. It made her feel lonely and out of place and wonder for the thousandth time why she had been born in such a land. Why anyone but the Indians and Mexicans, who belonged no place else, stayed there.

Her eyes were snagged by near movement.

Will moved over beside Grady and leaned back to make a cigarette. He belonged, she thought. Of all the white men she knew, William Graham, the little known man, belonged. It stood out in every line of his body; in the way he was even now topping off a cigarette and popping it into his mouth.

He was like an Apache in everything but color: in the sharp, restless impassivity of his eyes, the inscrutability of his face, even in his powerful shoulders and arms and compactly built, indestructible frame.

He wasn't tall; perhaps two or three inches under six feet, but he emanated a solid toughness. A strange, disconcerting fierceness lay dormant under his relaxed and deliberate way of handling himself.

Yes, Will Graham belonged in this land. Grady Stewart, owner of the trading post, didn't. It was breaking Grady. The lonely oppressiveness and the monstrous silences were pressing down on him. It showed in his churning, restless eyes, in the quick droop of his shoulders and in the long line of his upper lip, the way it turned downward more and more above the soft gristle of his mobile chin.

And even her own father, John Maxwell, who had died recently and whom she'd always thought of *as* Arizona, hadn't really belonged in the sense that Will Graham did. John had fought the land, the Mexicans, the Indians — fought everything — and had died fighting poverty hardest of all. Craggy old John had thought only in terms of force and defiance. He had built a rickety empire of cows and acres, with a gun and a hangrope. By force of character John Maxwell had wrenched a living out of Arizona, and in so doing he had buried a wife, an infant son, and left his daughter a legacy of thorns and bitterness. She had sold the cattle and horses before they dwindled away to nothing and the land she still owned was valueless. She worked for Grady Stewart and lived in one of the little adobes behind the trading post. She had known since she had come back from school and seen her father in a new light that Arizona would beat him in the end; and it had.

John Maxwell was gone and Arizona was still there, with the maddening patience of the desert, waiting to take it all back again as though John Maxwell's shadow had never darkened the land.

The difference between the two men, her father and Will Graham whom no one knew anything about, was simply that Maxwell had been strong and powerful and forceful. Will Graham was *patient* and strong and powerful. He was like Arizona; her father wasn't. It wasn't much of a difference, but it was enough.

The ragged village lay dormant under the violent mid-day heat. Little thick adobe hovels, never quite square, flat-roofed and with melancholy window-holes without glass, and wisps of dirty canvas at the doorways, hunkered indifferently along a crooked roadway. The road, about six hundred feet long, haphazardly made and unkempt, defined the limits of Melton, Arizona Territory, in 1881.

She looked from the ageless somnolence of the village to the desert beyond, and it lulled her. She smelt tobacco smoke and liked it. Stirring out of her heat-inspired lassitude, she threw a sidelong glance at Grady.

"Now'd be a good time to bring the books up on the pledges, wouldn't it, Grady?"

The trader continued his pointless stare into nowhere. "I reckon, Karen," he said tonelessly. "Any time."

She left them and walked across the ramada and into the cool, gloomy trading post with its endless spectrum of clashing color. Concho belts, turquoise-inlaid jewelry, massive silver bow-guards, piles of aromatic blankets, reed and willow baskets, all the private and public goods of Indians, sold, or pledged and awaiting redemption. Navaho, Pueblo, Mojave, Apache, Zuni — the culture and religion of desert Indians galore, was piled and hanging, heaped and stacked, in that one large adobe room with its low, smoke-stained ceiling.

It was a world that never failed to make her aware of the unbridgable difference between the dark, secretive, faintly frightening Indians who lived "out there somewhere" and herself. If there was a way to cross the abyss between white and Indian, she thought the only person who might ever achieve it was a man like Will Graham — a white Indian. A man who could understand Indians; one who didn't necessarily condone what they did but who understood why they did it.

Will stood now, watching a slab-sided Mexican dog ambling down the road; watching the little spurts of dun dust that jerked to life under his leathery pads. The silence was complete. The Mexicans were all indoors. They wouldn't come out until late afternoon. They'd sleep all day, or at least until the two-foot-thick walls of their mud houses couldn't resist the heat any longer. Then they'd come outside where it was cooler than inside, hunt a shady place and sleep some more.

Grady swore a grisly oath and rammed his hands deeper into his pockets so that his shoulders were dragged down still more.

"You know, Will, I wish someone'd come along and offer me half what I've got in this darned post."

Will saw the sheen of perspiration over Grady's cheekbones, the thrust and slant of his jaw and the discouragement plain on his face. He looked away and spat out his dead cigarette. "It's the heat, Grady. When December gets here you'll feel differently."

"December, nothing! Will, there's two seasons to this country. Heat like the hubs of hell and cloudbursts; that's all. You either melt for ten months or all of a sudden the clouds bank up, get blacker'n sin and dump a year's supply of water on you in two hours."

Will chuckled. It was a deep, soothing sound. "Arizona isn't the only place like that, Grady. New Mexico has its deserts too."

Grady considered that and perked up. He'd heard Will talk of New Mexico before. In a land where personal questions were taboo, a man pieced together things carelessly dropped. Over a year or two he came to certain conclusions about strangers. He'd known Will Graham since the day, eighteen months before, when he'd stepped down off his horse, another silent stranger to Melton. Since that day he'd tried to create a pattern for Will. New Mexico was as far as he'd ever gotten. Defeat claimed him easily now. He quit wondering and dropped back into his moody groove again.

"Heat, cloudbursts, and Apaches. The three seasons of Arizona."

"I'll take the heat," Will said dryly.

"I'll take the next stage out," Grady said. "Only I've got this darned trading post." He flicked a driblet of sweat off his long nose. "For all it'll make me this year I might as well go fishing — if there was any place to fish."

"I know a place," Will said, looking up at the towering, sere Galiuros. "There're trout up there twenty inches long, Grady. The water's as blue as turquoise. You catch them with a buckle-tongue. That's what I used when I found the place."

"Yeah, and if you get caught, instead of the fish, you wake up bald-headed."

"Oh, it won't always be like this."

"The devil it won't. What's here to draw people, Will, tell me that, will you?"

Will answered slowly, "This is good country, Grady, only you can't buck it. If you'll learn from the country you'll get along fine."

"Humph!"

Will chuckled again. "I mean it. The Indians know how to live here."

"Who wants to live like an Indian?"

Will's eyes sobered. "They live pretty well. The way to live out here is simply to adapt yourself. When the fishing's good, you fish. When the hunting's good, you hunt. When it's too hot, you hibernate. It's pretty simple, but when you do like John Maxwell did — fight everything and try to make the desert over into what you think it should be — why then you go under."

But Grady wasn't listening. He had straightened up and was staring southward, down through the sea of heat that shimmered over the country, toward the place where the barren old flanks of the Galiuros hunched low on the desert.

"Will, by golly, someone's coming!" The dumbfounded astonishment in his voice was a natural thing. There hadn't been a stage, or even a freighter, through Melton since the Apaches had gone out again. The whole breadth of Arizona was still and hushed and waiting. The land was under siege. No one traveled now. It had

16

nothing to do with the summer heat blast either — just Apaches!

Will looked. It was a top-buggy with riders around it. They were coming slowly. He could picture the way the horses looked; rib cages pumping for oxygen in the thin, blazing air, eyes red and nostrils caked and dry. He grunted and slitted his eyes, watching. Grady went across the swept earth of the ramada, poked his head inside the trading post and called to Karen.

Will was vastly puzzled. He counted seven outriders. Hardly enough to fight off Apaches, and yet they must have come over the unused old stage road, and he knew for a fact that Apache sentinels were high on the peaks along the way. Luck and stupidity might account for their survival. He couldn't think of anything else that would.

Karen was standing beside him. Her lips were parted a little, and the softness of her cheeks below the upsweep of her dark lashes struck him. He had seen her many times and, like Grady, had taken her for granted. Now it suddenly came over him that she was very pretty. He twisted to look back at the strangers. They were closer but seemed to move no faster. His mind stayed on Karen while his eyes measured the progress of the newcomers.

Until this moment Karen had seemed to belong to another world. He knew, of course, that it was Will Graham, not the girl or the country, that had made her seem that way to him before.

17

He had been a sick man when he had come to Melton. Not physically ill — he was as strong and durable as a bull — but sick inwardly. It had colored everything he had seen. All he had wanted then was secrecy and solitude. Everything had been grey and withered, but now the pull of this wild land had wrought its magic on him, and Karen Maxwell was part of it.

He thought of how he'd seen her looking at him, appraisingly, as though she wondered about him. And the forthright way she had accepted him, as Grady had, at face value. He thought, too, that she was supple and strong and quite handsome. And in the midst of these thoughts he saw the little wisp of dirty grey smoke go squirting skyward as though propelled by a gust of wind. He knew it wasn't the wind but the wetted blanket of an Indian jerked swiftly upward over a signal fire, high on the spiked ridge of the Galiuros.

They were watching, after all.

Karen didn't see it. He knew, because she turned when Grady came back, and spoke without mentioning it. "Grady? Are there any lemons left?"

"Lemons?" Grady said owlishly. "Oh, there're some in the springhouse, Karen. Lemonade? That's a good idea."

She left them, and Will watched her go with an odd look in his blue glance. Grady saw the gaze and smiled.

"Women are like that. I am thinking, 'Who are

they?' You think, 'How'd they make it?' She thinks, 'They'll be warm and want some lemonade.' " He laughed, and Will looked at him searchingly, saying nothing. It was good to hear Grady laugh. He hadn't often done it in the past year or so.

The buggy came so slowly, the last half-mile seemed to take hours. The horses were scarcely moving, true, but it was the deceptiveness of desert distances more than anything else that gave a false illusion of closeness. Grady made a cigarette to kill time. Will leaned against the adobe wall, hardly moving at all. When he spoke finally it showed that his mind had back-tracked.

"I can't understand how they did it, Grady. There's always a sentinel on the East Wall. There's another at Ambush Spring. There's one at the turnoff where they come up this way. I know that one's up there, because I saw his smoke a little while ago."

"Maybe they didn't want to jump them, Will. I know that doesn't make sense, but how else would they get through? There's not enough of them to fight off an attack. I count seven riders."

"Yeah," Will said softly, lost in thought. "Seven riders and at most, two in the buggy. Maybe three. Nine against the Lord alone knows how many Apaches that're slipping around this end of the desert. It beats me, Grady."

When the muted noise of the horsemen came, Mexican dogs appeared as though from the earth, stiff-legged, hackles up, barking excitedly in a sort of off-key concert of bedlam. That in turn brought Mexican heads to doors and windows; motionless, sweat-sheathed dark faces staring, as Will and Grady were, unbelievingly.

The buggy swung in toward the ramada of the trading post and the mounted men, all grey and streaked and dehydrated-looking, began to climb stiffly down and stamp away the layers of dun dust. A horse blew his nose and the buggy creaked. Two men got down, walked around to the ramada and went up where Grady and Will were standing. One, lean and tall and cadaverous-looking, with skin pulled over his face like the head of a drum, nodded.

"Is this Melton?"

Grady nodded, saying nothing. Will used the moment to appraise the strangers. The lean man had small grey eyes as hard and as dry as bleached stones. The other man, shorter, heavier, was dripping with perspiration. He had a brooding, baleful look and seemed to be awed by the country they had just come over. His eyes lingered on it.

"Good." He extended his hand toward Grady. "I'm Judge Curtin. This is Mister Allen."

Grady pumped the hands and introduced Will Graham. Karen came out with the lemonade. It was tart and eye-watering, but no wise person drank it sweetened on the desert. Grady introduced her, too. The lean man's smile was quick and civil. Allen's nod was almost a bow, and his eyes lingered.

Judge Curtin swung back with his lemonade in a thin hand. "Mister Stewart, they told me at Tucson I could get housing from you for the men I brought with me." The little grey eyes probed Grady's face.

"Well, I suppose we can fix something up, Judge," Grady said slowly. "This time of the year it's better to sleep outside than inside, though."

"I believe that," Curtin said with a bird-like nod of his head. He turned and looked at the horsemen lounging in the shade over by Will's horse. "Tom, come here a moment, will you?"

A burly, sweat-drenched man broke away from the other riders and stamped over to the ramada. Will's appraisal was swift and simple — gunman. It was written in every line of the newcomer's face, in his stance and stare and butt-forward, tied-down gun.

"This is Tom Elmore, gentlemen. He's head of my riders."

They shook hands. Elmore's eyes flicked over them one at a time and stayed longest on Karen, then lifted to the judge's face with a dryly questioning glance. Curtin nodded toward Grady.

"Mister Stewart can show you where you'll stay, Tom." He glanced at Grady. "Would you?"

Grady nodded, a little more slowly this time, and walked back where the others were waiting, with Tom Elmore at his side.

Judge Curtin glanced at the buggy and team.

"Mike, will you put up the horses?"

Allen straightened with a suppressed sigh and walked away. Will wondered at the quick, soft way Curtin spoke, and how he was obeyed instantly whenever he spoke. The judge's lemonade wasn't half gone when he looked over at Will. It was like being used for a window. The grey eyes had penetrating power.

"Mister Graham, I can see you're wondering how we made it."

Will nodded his head without looking at the judge. Mike Allen, instead of leading the team the little way he had to go, was driving the buggy toward the sagging barn that once had housed John Maxwell's horses.

Curtin's gaze grew motionless, studying Will's profile. "We were lucky, just plain lucky. At Tucson they said we'd never make it."

"I would've said the same thing," Will said, watching Karen's face, seeing the faintly disturbed look there.

"So would I, normally," Judge Curtin said. "But Mike and I went over the dispatches. They showed the bulk of the raiders south of here. It looked as though there was some build-up in progress down toward the border. That being true, we decided we'd make a run for it."

"You traveled mostly at night. Is that it?"

"Yes, as long as we could; then we just hightailed it." The drumhead face cracked into an incongruous smile. "You could tell that from the look of the horses, I imagine."

"I thought you must have," Will said. "It's good you made it." Will turned and looked at Curtin. His blue gaze wasn't especially friendly. There was something about Curtin — his way of giving orders — his confidence — something; it held a man off. Will glanced over at Karen again. She was regarding the judge strangely, the faintly disturbed look stronger now. He couldn't help but feel slight amusement at her steady, easily read expression. "Karen," he said. She started a little and swung to look at him. "Let's go inside. Cooler in there."

They trooped into the big room of the post and Judge Curtin killed time looking around. Will went to the table Grady had built against the wall, and dropped down on the bench. Karen sat down beside him and raised her eyebrows. He showed a little glint of humor and shrugged. They fell into an awkward silence, waiting. It lasted until Grady and Mike Allen came back. The trader's face was furrowed in a worried way. Allen, damper, more wilted-looking than before, hesitated briefly and sprawled on the bench. Grady stood uncertainly, waiting for the judge. When Curtin crossed the room, Grady sat down. He wasted no time on preliminaries.

"Well, Judge, you're a long way from the settlements. What brings you out here now? I mean, this is a heck of a time of the year to be traveling, what with the Indians out again and all."

Curtin stood with his thin legs spread and his emptied lemonade glass in his hand. He seemed to be enjoying this moment. Will's mental reservations concerning the man grew. Mike Allen seemed resigned to something, as though this were an old, old drama to him.

"Mister Stewart, I'm here in a private capacity, not an official one. I have a law practice on the side, you understand, and one of my clients has retained me to do a rather unusual service for him." Curtin stopped there, his steady eyes probing Grady, taking his measure and sifting through what he saw.

"Three weeks ago a family of Easterners named Thorndike left Tucson on their way to the Coast. There was Mister and Missus Thorndike and two youngsters — both boys. One lad was nine, the other twelve. Several days ago they passed through your part of the country on a Merrill-Lynch stage."

Will's eyes flickered. He had seen that stage. Quick as a flash Curtin saw his slight movement and swung his head a little to stare directly at Will. The hard glance was appraising again, and thoughtful. Will thought he was going to speak to him, but Curtin swung back toward Grady again.

"The parents were killed, as you may have heard, Mister Stewart, but we have reason to believe the little boys weren't. At least no one's found their bodies."

Grady slumped a little and nodded. "They

don't always kill kids," he said. "In fact, if they're husky kids — and boys — they take them along a lot of the times." He turned toward Will. "Isn't that right, Will?"

"Right." Will was watching the judge. He found himself revising his first appraisal of the man. Whatever it was about him that repelled Will, he admitted that Curtin was quick, and probably very smart.

The judge's head moved back a trifle. His gaze fell on Will again. "From Mister Stewart's question to you, Mister Graham, I infer you know Indians. Am I wrong?"

"Not entirely," Will said carefully. "I don't know Indians, but I've been around Apaches a little."

Curtin's smile came swiftly, and just as swiftly died. "Good. Fine. That's exactly what I'd hoped for." He shot a long look at Allen as though in triumph. "My entire strategy has been based on two things, gentlemen. One, that we could get here. Two, that once here, we'd find a native who could help us do what has to be done."

"Like what?" Will asked bluntly.

"Get those two boys back."

Will let his gaze slide away from Curtin. He grew silent and stayed that way so long Grady and Karen thought he wasn't going to speak at all. Then he said, "Who's your client, Judge?"

"The uncle of the boys. The only living relative they have left now. He's the brother of the man who was killed."

"He didn't waste any time getting things rolling, did he?"

"No. He's a wealthy and influential man. He hired me right away to employ an army if necessary, and get those boys back."

"The army would be the gunmen you brought with you?"

"Yes."

"And now you want to live at Melton and hire me to guide your army after Apaches?"

"Yes."

Will swung his head and looked ironically at Grady. Karen saw the darkness seeping into his glance. So did Mike Allen, the stocky, melting man sitting beyond Grady on the wall-bench.

"Well?"

Will looked up at Curtin without answering. He knew what it was that he didn't like about Judge Curtin: arrogance. He dropped his glance and looked at the far wall. Curtin wasn't the kind of a man who would understand the delicacy of what was required, or the danger.

"Mister Stewart?"

"To start with," Will said quietly, "we don't Mister one another in Melton. My name's Will. Stewart's is Grady." He paused, watching for a reaction. There was none.

"You've brought seven gunmen. That's fine — only they wouldn't make a dent against the Apaches living around here. Not a dent."

"There are some of the best gunmen on the

frontier among them."

"I don't doubt it," Will said, remembering the hard, capable, violent look of Tom Elmore. "But they won't be fighting in barrooms. They can outshoot Apaches, probably, but they'll never see an Indian to shoot at. That's the first stumbling block. The next one is that you'd need at least fifty more just like them — maybe twice that number."

"I can get them."

"I don't doubt it," Will said dryly, softly. "But you don't dare fight Apaches, Judge. The first time you crowded them they'd take those two boys by the ankles and smash their heads against a rock. They do that when they want a breather: kill their prisoners and lay them out neatly for those pursuing to find, and stop to bury." Will's voice made a musical pattern broken only by the sound of a big old wall clock.

"That's my first and primary objection to your strategy, Judge. The second objection I have is this. So far, Melton's been safe. We haven't bothered the Apaches and they haven't bothered us. If you use Melton as headquarters and fight from here, the hostiles'll come down here some dawn and turn this village inside out."

"We'll be prepared for that, Mister Graham."

"Will's the name. No, you won't. Your seven gunmen won't stand a chance." Will made a slight gesture with one hand. "I know they're good. I can see that. You know they are, too. What you don't know is that the Apaches are better, especially on their home ground."

For half a minute no one said anything; then Allen, from his place down the bench, spoke directly to Will. "How would you go about this thing, Mister Graham?"

He fished for his tobacco sack and began to manufacture a brown-paper cigarette with slow methodicalness. "I'd find out first if the boys are alive. After that . . ."

"How?" Curtin interrupted.

Will lit up and exhaled. "Ask around — how else?"

Curtin didn't reply. His grey eyes were fixed to Will's face with a dry intentness.

"I'd find out if they were alive; then I'd try to ransom them."

"I'm prepared to go along with that," Curtin said.

It irritated Will so he kept his head lowered, his face in the shadows of his hat brim, and smoked.

Allen was nodding his head in an abstract, unconscious way, his eyes baleful and ironic-looking. "Could you do that, Will? Could you talk to them?"

"I suppose so."

Mike Allen looked up swiftly at Judge Curtin. The judge, if aware of his friend's look, ignored it in his close scrutiny of Will.

"Will you?"

"Yes. I'll see what I can do," Will said. "But I want your word you'll keep every man-jack you

28

brought with you in the village. If you send them out or let them go nosing around, it'll endanger the boys' lives and mine too."

"How long will it take?" Curtin asked sharply.

Will shrugged. "I can't say. It depends on how long it takes me to find the Indians. Maybe a week. Maybe a month."

"Mister Thorndike wants action," Curtin said.

Will looked up quickly. "Mister Thorndike can wait," he said tartly, "or he can do it himself. Or he can let you do it your way and he'll never see his nephews again." To soften his words, he added, "This won't be a picnic, Judge, either way, your way or my way. If you want me to try it on those terms I'll do my best. If not . . ." He shrugged again.

The silence came back and Karen saw quick distaste flash across Judge Curtin's face. She looked down at Will. He wasn't looking at Curtin at all. His gaze was moodily fixed on the far wall again.

"It's feasible," Mike Allen said tentatively, looking at Curtin.

The judge seemed to arrive at a decision. He leaned and put his lemonade glass on the table. "All right, Mister Graham. We'll do it your way. I hope it doesn't take any month, though."

Will was thinking of the little signal smoke he had seen on the jagged spires of the Galiuros. He didn't think it'd take even a week, but he didn't say so. He wanted a lot of time — in case.

"Mister Stewart, can I have a word with you outside? There're the financial arrangements to be made for quartering my men."

Grady got up and walked out of the room ahead of Curtin. Mike Allen was gazing at Will and Karen. He looked uncomfortable. Neither seemed aware of his presence. He got up, mumbled something, and went through the doorway that led to the ramada.

Karen moved down the bench and looked up into Will's face. "He's unusual, isn't he?"

Will smashed out his cigarette against the back wall and dropped it. There was hard humor in his voice when he answered, looking into her face.

"Unusual? That's a very nice name to call it."

"I feel something about him, Will."

"I reckon you do. Men feel it with other men even quicker than women do."

"What is it?"

"Well, it's dislike, for one thing. It's normal reaction to a stuffed shirt, for another. Judge Curtin's wearing his judgeship and his arrogance like a coat of mail. You're supposed to be dazzled by it; bounce off it sort of, Karen."

"But you'll go, won't you?"

"Sure. I'll go. It'll take about two days to get ready, though. You can't run out calling names for a thing like this."

Chapter 2

She studied his profile thoughtfully. The deeply set eyes seemed to be watching a dozen places at once.

"Did you say it looked like there were two couples on the stage, Will?"

"Yes, but it could have been two boys and two adults. All I had to go by was pieces of torn clothing."

"You don't think the Indians killed the boys?"

"No."

"They took them?"

"Yes."

Her mouth tightened. "Why don't you want to talk about it?"

"For the same reason you wouldn't, Karen, if you'd seen the signs around — the blue-tailed flies drinking the blood that looked like blackberry jelly."

That shocked her into silence. For a while she sat there with her hands like dead birds, limp in her lap; then she got up and walked away.

Will didn't move for a long time, not until after Grady came back and crossed the room with a brooding look and dropped down beside him.

"What do you think, Will?"

"Probably the same thing you do. Curtin's a stuffed shirt, a little Napoleon. He's got an army and a big fat fee coming, and some sort of glory if he can get the kids back."

"Oh, him," Grady said. "I didn't mean him. I meant can you talk to the Indians — get the kids back, maybe?"

"I can try," Will said. "I don't know any more what's ahead than you do." He turned with a tiny smile. "If I knew, maybe I wouldn't even try, Grady."

"What I don't like is what'll happen to Melton if he pulls the plug and lets those gunmen loose."

"He said he wouldn't," Will reminded him. "He'd better keep his word, too."

Grady slumped, locked his fingers together and stared at the floor. What he said startled Will. "Two little boys."

Will got up abruptly and strolled outside to the ramada. There was a barrel-chair out there and a bench. Mike Allen was wedged into the chair. Ignoring him, Will sprawled on the bench looking out into the late afternoon where the sun was a bloody disc lowering itself gingerly against the spike-toothed mountains to the west. The desert lay hushed. There was a wild, sad beauty to it. He raised his eyes under the overhang of his hat brim to the high peaks, bare and forbidding-looking. He knew of an ancient spiraling trail that wound aloft with a hundred ambushing places along its perilous lift. The Apache Trail; old as time itself, highroad for the furtive fighters

of the farthest frontier — the desert country. He dropped his glance and thought of the way there, of the scattered evidences of violence to be passed; the skeleton of a long-dead horse with the black-curled leather that once had been a saddle. Macabrely, the latigos still held a horse-hair cincha where once a belly had been.

The sun was lower now, in a spotless sky frayed a little at the far outer edges. Mike Allen seemed carved of soft tallow. He was as still as Will was.

He thought of other things too, in that dying part of the day; of dim faces, ghost-like, out of his past, of scenes and sayings and events. Little scraps of things that had made up his life before he had lost himself in the solitudes around Melton. He pushed them back with a ruthless-ness Karen wouldn't have thought him capable of, and threw his glance out where the rocky slopes dipped low in a hunched over salute to the barren land beyond.

Mike Allen left when someone beat a triangle. Will watched his heavy stride, barely aware of his passing. Of himself he thought that a man might do great or foolish things, but fate would give him another chance some day. If he was a fool, he'd have a chance to be a better man or a bigger fool. If he had been great, she would give him a chance to be greater, probably. He swore softly and got up, crossed to the edge of the ramada and leaned against an upright post, watching the shadows come.

He was still there an hour later, looking up at the star-splashed grandeur of an Arizona summer night. The big old moon, solid gold-looking because of the dust in the air, was almost close enough to touch.

He heard the rustle of footfalls and turned. It was Karen Maxwell. He watched her stroll over closer. She saw him and hesitated.

"Good evening, Will."

"Oh, it's you. Good evening."

She walked over near him, seeing the way he leaned on the old post, his face softened by the night light, but what he said when she was beside him was brutal. It was as though he were taking up where they had left off earlier.

"Did you ever see kids that've had their brains bashed out against a tree trunk?"

"No."

"I have. They do it to slow down pursuit — or if the kids get sick or cry a lot."

Karen sniffed. "Does talking about it please you?"

"No. I didn't think you understood this afternoon."

She had no trouble imagining what he had been like as a boy.

"Beautiful night."

"Yes," he said. "I like the evenings and the dawns."

"I do too."

He made a cigarette and lit it and looked out at the vastness, the ghostly grey silhouettes of

mountains. "I like the days, too," he said.

"I know you do."

He looked around at her. "How do you know?"

She shrugged. "You're that kind of a man."

His voice sounded amused. "What do you know about men?"

She answered with a little flare of spirit. "I was just about raised by men. I'm glad of it, too, because this is a man's country. I understand men and I understand the country."

He started to say something, checked himself and said something else instead. "It's a good thing you do, because if you didn't you'd hate it."

"No," she said gravely. "I'd never hate it because I love silence and distance and this is one part of the world that'll never change very much."

"Not even in the tomorrows?" he asked, not quite mocking her. "Not even when the Apaches are tamed?"

"No, because there'll never be many people here," she said without looking at him. "It isn't a land that attracts people. Oh, a certain kind — but not people generally speaking. And there are no tomorrows here anyway. Just today."

He puzzled over that without speaking or looking around at her again. When he had been silent a long time, she spoke again.

"The judge's army turned in early — for their kind."

"What kind is that?" he asked, looking at her again in a strange way.

"Oh — border types. Gunmen, drinkers — you know what I mean."

"I guess I do at that."

"Walk with me," she said abruptly.

They walked side by side down the dusty roadway. The wonderful coolness was a blessing on the land. It had a dry, musty fragrance all its own. They stopped at a decaying little chapel, with an askew cross made of manzanita limbs atop its mud roof.

She sat on the steps, and he lowered himself beside her and ran his legs out full length and gazed at his dust-furred boots.

"How can anyone hate Arizona on a night like this?" she asked.

"Grady can," he said without looking up. "A lot of people could. If I'd had to come here, I might have hated it myself."

"But you didn't have to; you came because you wanted to."

"Not exactly."

"Well, you had to in the sense that you had to go somewhere, I understand that, Will. But you didn't have to come to Melton."

"No," he said very quietly.

She took her courage in both hands then. "Was it a girl, Will?"

He was silent for so long she was afraid he wouldn't answer. Then he said, "Yes."

"I knew it was."

"Did you?" There was no mistaking the soft irony that time. He still stared at his boots, his face blank.

"Yes. You're that kind of a man."

Then he looked over at her. There was an unaccustomed sternness in his gaze. "That's the second time you've said that. What kind of a man am I?"

With a sweet candidness, she turned and met his gaze with her own. "Will you find the Indians, Will?"

He dropped his glance and put annoyance aside. "I reckon so. I've found them before."

"Aren't you afraid they'll kill you?"

"Yes, but if it's the right ones they won't, though."

"How can you be sure?"

"I can't. That's why I said it might take a month. An Apache has no concept of time, Karen. Today or tomorrow or a month from now, it's all the same to him. Time to an Apache is the wait between drinks of water or between full moons. That's all. When I'm out there I feel the same way about it. It's nothing. If you hurry, nature'll do what an Apache might not do — kill you."

"So you'll take all the time and care you have to, to find the right Indians and do what you have to do."

"Yes."

She moved a little. Her dress made a soft

sound like rustling leaves. She put both arms around her drawn up knees and gazed up at the sky.

"Did you finish college, Will?"

His head snapped up as though she'd struck him. She was still watching the heavens and the little quarter-moon touched her face with a milky light. She said it in so impersonal a manner the sting was taken away. What captured his glance was the way the light showed the strength, the even beauty and the calmness of her features.

"Yes, I finished."

"I didn't."

"I know; your father died."

But she wasn't thinking of her father or her incompleted education. She was thinking of Will and the other woman. He wouldn't be hard to hurt, she knew that, but he'd die before he'd show his pain. She sighed and rested her chin on her knees, thinking of the woman, whoever she was.

"When you get over your bitterness, Will, you'll saddle up and ride away."

He straightened very erect. "Karen, you have a nasty knack of startling people."

She ignored it. "Won't you?"

"I don't know. Anyway, I'm not bitter."

She didn't contradict him. She was too tactful for that. "You think of her, Will," she said softly. For the first time in her life, she hated someone enough to despise her, and in a way that was illogical too, because she didn't even know the woman's name or what she looked like or where she lived. She lifted her head, turned it and looked straight at him. His eyes were shades darker.

"Karen, don't wonder about me too much.

"We're friends," he said, not sure what that meant. "In this country that's enough. Pasts don't count for much."

"You want me at arm's length?"

"Well, yes."

She heard the deep gust of breath come out of him and looked back at the sky again. "All right," she said, and for a while they were perfectly relaxed and silent. Then she spoke again. "Will, I've changed my mind."

"What about?" he asked, eyeing her askance.

"I don't think you'll ever leave Melton. Now walk me home."

He did, hearing the slush-slush-slush of their feet in the powdery dust, and at the doorway she reached out and touched his broad, big-knuckled hand.

"I'm not ashamed of my curiosity, Will, but I apologize for it."

He left her in the darkness and strode back toward Grady's trading post. Inside, the trader was looking petulantly at the big plate of cold beans.

"Well, fine time to show up for supper, Will."

"Supper?"

"Yes, supper. You didn't eat with Curtin's

crew and you didn't eat with the Mexicans — so where would you eat?"

"I forgot to," Will said with a slow smile. "I plumb forgot to."

"Likely," Grady said. "Well, there it is. It's cold. You'll probably get a bellyache. Serves you right."

While Will ate Grady brought out a thick, dusty bottle of Mexican wine and filled two glasses with it. He drank his in one draught and refilled the glass, avoiding Will's eyes, sank down on a chair and fished for his tobacco sack. Will looked at the swirling sediment in the amber wine and went back to eating.

"I mind my own business," Grady said suddenly. Will carefully laid aside his fork and looked closely at Grady's face. He hadn't noticed the flush before. Now he did. The wine wasn't the first drink Grady had taken since nightfall.

"I mind my own business, but I'm sure curious about one thing, Will."

"What?"

Grady turned a wide stare at Will. "How did you happen to get on speaking terms with Apaches, anyway?"

"How? Well, I was fishing at that spot I told you about, Grady, and I ran across a buck Indian with a running sore as big as a 'dobe dollar. He was pretty sick, chanting his death song. That's how I found him, by the noise. He was half delirious."

"And?"

"I knocked him over the head with my pistol, cut into the sore and dug out a mesquite thorn a half-inch long that was buried about two inches inside and working farther in. After that it was pretty simple. I used a little of my salt, boiled some water and kept him down for a couple of days — and that was that."

"That was that, with one buck," Grady said, "but how about the rest of 'em?"

"Oh, he passed the word around when I let him go."

"You mean you stayed up there fishing?"

Will grinned at Grady's incredulousness. "It was like this. If I'd run they'd've caught me. I was too far back in to get out with much of a start. I stayed. They put me up for a day and a night; then, the first thing I knew, I had six more patients. After that . . ."

"I see. What were they?"

"Mescaleros."

"Humph!" Grady sniffed. "Next to Chiricahuas, Mescaleros are the worst of them all."

"Oh, I wouldn't say that," Will said slowly, watching Grady smoke and drink wine.

"Well, I don't care. I do business with them too — when I can. But you know how people are, especially Mexicans. They've got the most fertile imaginations on earth, and they're more scairt of Apaches than God himself." He looked over at Will and made an elaborate shrug, then refilled Will's wine glass.

Will watched the swirling sediment and spoke absently. "I don't do any business with them," he said, "but they're human."

Grady looked shocked. "Apaches human?"

"Sure. Grady, you're ignorant. You do business with them and don't try to understand them at all."

"Not much," Grady dissented. "Most of my business is with Pueblos, Navahos, a few wandering Cocomaricopas and what-not, but few cussed Apaches."

"Oh?" Will said, his voice on a rising note and his eyebrows climbing a little. "Where'd that Mexican crucifix come from?" He pointed to the beautiful, tarnished rosary with its fabulously wrought image in the center in massive gold overlay. "You didn't buy that from any Navaho."

"I said I get a few," Grady said defensively without looking up to frown at the crucifix. "I'm here to buy, Will, not pass judgment."

"But you could take an interest in your customers."

Grady puffed out his lips and drew them down a little. "I reckon," he said. "Have it your way. All I say is that Apaches ought to be wiped out or sent a long way off so's business could be run like it should be, and everyone wouldn't have to sleep with two pistols and a shotgun every couple of years." He poured more of the muddy wine. "If things don't straighten out pretty cussed quick I'm going to pull out of this country so fast you won't even see the dust."

Will pushed his plate away and examined the wine moodily. He thought Grady should get away, at least for a while: go down to Tucson or over to Prescott in the Mogollons or out to California. If he didn't, and if the blockade of outlying settlements like Melton wasn't lifted pretty soon, Grady Stewart was going to break.

"Customers," Grady said suddenly, violently. "Copper-bellies." He turned his flushed face and shining eyes toward Will. "You have any idea how much I've got tied up in pledges to 'em, Will? According to the books, by golly, I've got two thousand in cash tied up in that junk!" He waved a hand backwards to indicate the rows and rows of jewelry, the piles of worn saddles; the pathetic treasures of Indiandom.

Will said nothing. He stretched out and looked down at his boots. Grady Stewart was farther along than he had thought.

Liquor and loneliness, Will decided. The two things that have killed more men on the desert than anything else ever has — Apaches included.

He got up and took his hat in one hand and looked down at Grady. "How'd you like to take this trip with me and leave Karen here to run the post?"

Grady looked appalled. "Are you crazy? Not on your life I wouldn't." Then his face relaxed. "There might be some buck out there who thought I'd robbed 'em in a trade sometime."

Will chuckled and bobbed his head. "Might be

at that. Well, I'll bed down on the ramada. See you in the morning."

"Sure. Say, Will, I almost forgot to tell you. Judge Curtin told me to tell you he'd pay you three dollars a day while you were out."

It wasn't the pay. No rider got more than a third of that. It was Curtin, the man who'd made the offer. "Tell him to use it to buy hobbles with."

"Hobbles?"

"Yeah, hobbles to keep his tough gunmen in Melton with while I'm gone."

He went back outside and heard music coming from a Mexican hovel south of the trading post. It had a sad and stirring quality. He listened a while, then went to his horse, put him in Grady's private faggot corral and forked him a lot of Grady's sweet-grass hay. Lugging his bedroll back around to the ramada, he bedded down. His last thoughts were of the questions Karen had plied him with. He said, very softly but aloud, "You — of all people — you know better than that." Then he fell asleep.

The hour was late, later than he had thought. He knew he had slept late when the pale sunlight dragged pink fingers across his eyes and woke him. He felt cheated and logy and lay there for a little while, watching the land stir to another day. It was the same as it always was, nothing changed. Then he understood what she had meant:

"There are no tomorrows."

He stirred, groped for his boots, tugged them on and stood up. She was right. It was always today on the desert. Yesterday was gone never to return and tomorrow never came. Today was here and now, because nothing changed; the dawns, the days, the nights, the mountains or the desert or the distance. He ran a hand through his coppery hair and made a wry face. Pretty abstract for such an early hour. He went around in back where the wash basin and soap were.

He and Grady had a bean breakfast with coffee that would have floated a horseshoe. While they were cleaning up the plates Judge Curtin came into the outer room and called out. Grady didn't miss a swipe with his feed-sack dishcloth.

"In here."

Curtin came through the door hanging. His grey eyes flickered swiftly over Will. He worried up a smile and spoke with cryptic geniality.

"Good morning, gentlemen. Mister Graham, will you leave today?"

"I will." He left it there, without amplification.

"You will." Curtin made it sound like a minor explosion. "Did you plan on leaving today?"

"Yes, but not until afternoon."

"Oh? I thought the dawn would be best."

"It would be," Will agreed, "except that I've got a horse to reshoe and some jerky and flour to round up."

"I can have one of my boys shoe your horse, if it'll help any."

"It won't," Will said bluntly. "I'd better do it myself. A lame horse is a risk I don't want to take."

Curtin seemed undecided. Grady was worrying dried beans off a plate with a cracked thumbnail. He seemed preoccupied. The judge's bright eyes switched from Grady's back to Will's face. His smile didn't come again.

"I suppose Mister Stewart told you of my payment offer."

"He did. You can keep it or, better yet, give it to Miss Maxwell." Curtin's eyes fixed themselves on Will's impassive face. "It isn't the money. I'd just rather do this without pay."

"I'm being paid, Will."

"That's your business. This isn't mine."

A strained silence settled for a fraction of a second; then Judge Curtin nodded. "All right. Miss Maxwell gets it then." He turned and grasped the curtain over the doorway. "Mister Stewart, do you stock whiskey?"

Grady answered before he turned. "No. Not for sale, Judge. Not allowed to on an Indian post."

"Yes, of course. I thought you might handle it for the white customers."

Grady smiled crookedly. "I don't get a dozen of those a year, Judge. Sorry."

Curtin left and Will finished wiping the crockery cups and hung them on bent nails and tossed the damp cloth over a string behind the cookstove. "Make me a bundle of jerky and flour

46

and canned stuff, will you?"

"Sure, I'll fetch it down to the old barn."

Will took a set of #2 cold shoes from the keg in the outer room, a handful of #4 nails, and led his horse into the coolness of the tumble-down Maxwell barn and shod him. The sweat came quickly in spite of the shade. He had to flick it off his nose a dozen times before he was finished, and before Grady showed up with some bundles that he forced into Will's saddlebags. By then it was a little before noon. They stood in the door-way of the barn looking out at the heat-lashed land.

Grady grumbled under his breath and spat dryly. "It's worth ten times what he offered, I'd say."

"Well, I don't just know how you'd charge a man for a thing like this, Grady. How much is a life worth, anyway?"

"He'll get plenty."

"Don't you like him? You'll make more off him and his gunmen crew than you'd make off Indians in six months. You were crying about business. I'd say this was the chance you've been waiting for."

"I'm not squawking," Grady grumbled. "It's — well —"

"I'll stay out longer if you want me to." Will looked over at the trader blandly. "I had no idea you were such an avaricious cuss, Grady."

"Oh, go to the devil." Grady didn't have a morose look exactly. It was more an expression

47

of tension. Finally he blurted out, "I don't like it, Will. Not any of it. Not just your part in it but all of it. Suppose you don't make it. He'll send those killers out and the Apaches'll come down here and pull Melton apart."

"I know that. What can you do about it? He's here and he isn't likely to leave until he has things his way. He's that type."

"Well," Grady said sullenly, "I don't know what we can do, but I know cussed well there's going to be trouble come out of this, sure as God made daylight." He turned and leveled a long look at Will. "And you be careful, Will. Darned careful."

Will watched the trader walk back up toward the post. There was a hidden shaft of amusement in his blue gaze. He made a cigarette and smoked it. When his horse had finished his bait of barley, he snuffed out the cigarette, slipped on the bridle, flicked up the split reins and toed in the stirrup. He took a long, deep breath of the barn's coolness and nudged his horse.

The sun was like the core of a dynamite blast when he rode out into it. It struck him squarely on the shoulders. He heard the muffled sound of his horse's hooves in the thick dust and fastened his slitted eyes on the desert ahead of him. He went past the trading post without looking at it.

Off in the east there were mountain peaks, bare and sharp. There was no reflection and no shade; just heat and silence and an abysmal hush that hung over everything. Behind him Melton crouched low on the burnished land, making itself inconspicuous. The adobes looked like mud cakes seen from a distance. He looked back just once. After that he kept his head forward and his eyes moving. He breathed deeply, feeling the need for more oxygen than there was in the hot atmosphere.

He felt the merciless heat waves. The cordillera ahead seemed miles closer than it was. There was a faint sheen of warmth radiating out from the bare rocky walls. It had a shimmering blue-greyness to it as though the heat itself came from those granite mountains.

Farther down the land, Will and his horse, damp with salt-sweat, rode where there was nothing to see but desert; a speck moving painfully. Melton far behind wasn't even a mirage. He swung a little westward, to skirt the base of the looming mountains, trailing over country that was soft enough to retain the imprint of his passage indefinitely. Late in the evening when the swollen sun was pouring out blood red fury in a descending rage, he came around the angle of the Galiuros and followed them northward.

From here on was Apacheria.

Long before the late twilight died out stubbornly and while the hidden sun still shot reflected light banners down over the land, he sought for, and found, a little swale to make his dry camp in.

The methods of making a camp were rudimentary and mechanical. He used one of the split reins to fashion a figure-eight horse hobble. He didn't light a cooking fire but ate what he found in his pack. After that he curled up on top of his saddle blanket and went to sleep.

He slept longer than he intended to and wasn't astride again until two or three hours before sunup. This would be the longest day. In a way he dreaded it. In another way, he looked forward to its end eagerly, for thirty miles ahead was the mountain pool he'd told Grady about. But it was the unseen nearness of peril that caught hold of him and kept him alert even after the scalding sun was at work. He felt no weariness even when the hours went trudging on.

It was possible that the sentinel who had signalled the coming of Curtin's crew hadn't seen him. It was more likely that he had. Whether he had or hadn't, Will had just one thin chance to rely on. He had started early enough to make tracking him a tedious and wearing process. As long as he held close to the flanks of the Galiuros there wasn't much risk of being seen from above.

Tracking him would be easy, but they would have had to wait until daylight, and that was the thing he was gambling on now. Let them come, so long as they didn't get closer than sight.

The fishing hole was in the Mescalero country of Juan Soldado. John Soldier's band of Mescaleros knew Will. If he had trailers and they weren't Mescaleros of Soldier's band, he was in danger, but somehow the peril didn't seem too real, for Juan Soldado had told him that he didn't allow any marauding around his rancheria. He wanted it quiet and peaceful there. For that reason Melton had never been attacked. For that reason, also, Will felt no imminence of danger beyond the normal peril he always faced when traveling through strange or hostile country.

The heat became unbearable in the afternoon, and he had to ride away from the Galiuros, farther out into the desert, and risk being seen from the pinnacles overhead. The yoke of his shirt had a familiar stiffness that chafed his flesh. He knew without looking that white salt crystals from his perspiration were caked there, like particles of fine ice.

Up ahead a mirage danced eerily. It was a river flowing among cottonwoods and red-bud willows. He smiled crookedly and laughed.

He watched the mirage, sucked a little pebble and rode with his eyes almost closed all through the afternoon. Just before the funnel mouth of a bleak canyon loomed off on his right, he reined back over against the mountain again, dismounted and worked his panting way up on a little outcropping of red-hot granite. There he hunkered like an ungainly, wingless buzzard, watching his back trail.

He shifted his feet often because the stones burned right through his soles, but he held his slitted stare, motionless and waiting. He watched until he could hear the slugging of his heart and feel the heat-tortured coursing of his blood inside his eardrums; then he was satisfied. No one was following.

He went back to the listless horse, swung up heavily and resumed his way. The funnel of the canyon was literally swimming with heat waves. He rode directly into them, and the stifling atmosphere was deadly. His horse shook its head in a lethargic way, but kept on going.

The land began to rise a little and footing became surer. There wasn't too much of the shifting, spongy desert dust underfoot now. The air cooled after a half a mile and up ahead, erect and majestic, was a pine tree. It sent out a tangy smell that was like a benediction after the brimstone stink of the hot country. Will smiled at the old tree and passed it by. It was his foremost landmark.

When he felt the ground leveling off he relaxed. The horse picked up energy too. There was a damp smell in the air; an invigorating freshness.

Up beyond the thin stand of pine and fir he came to the pool. An upland freshet spent its first strength there, where the willows and great grey boulders protected the tiny lake from the lower desert heat and fury. Below the pool, where the run-off was, lay a wedge of dark canyon.

Juan Soldado's band had lived here for centuries. Will got down with aching legs and shook his head to clear it. The Apaches couldn't have found a better spot anywhere. They knew it, too, for they kept this upland hideout a secret, guarding it jealously, and burying their dead up among the pines and firs.

He off-saddled and hobbled his horse and watched it crow-hop down to where the tender grass was and nuzzle the pool, sending out ever widening circlets of ripples. Then he lay down full length atop a big shady boulder and looked into the pool. He lay like that for an undisturbed hour, just looking, before he rolled up on one side, fished in a pants pocket, found a shiny half-dollar, pitched it with great care so that it landed almost in the middle of the pool, and watched some more.

He didn't have to wait so long that time.

Grey-black glistening shapes came gliding curiously. Against the silvery gravel at the bottom of the pool he could make them out easily. Trout, the biggest, fattest mountain trout he had seen in many years.

He sighed and pressed his chin down on the rock watching them.

Chapter 3

He awoke the following morning feeling refreshed. He also awoke surprised, for there wasn't an Apache in sight sitting idly, waiting, as there had been the other times he had been here. He washed and ate, looked for his horse and found the animal full and drowsing. He went back to his saddlebags, rummaged for the carefully honed buckle tongue he had long ago fashioned into a serviceable fish hook, checked the little ball of line for weaknesses, and threw into the clear pool baited with a tiny piece of salted jerky.

Sitting there in a shady spot, unmoving, as still as the tree he leaned against, his mind worked slowly. It was a little odd that the sentinels hadn't sent word out that someone was back in the hills. It preyed on his mind. After he had caught seven big trout and packed them carefully in moss in his saddle bags, he broke camp and started up the gentle slope of the country toward where he knew Soldado's permanent camp was.

He stopped on a grassy meadow once, and made a small fire out in plain sight. When it was burning well he threw a handful of pine needles on it, held his hat over the thickly billowing smoke for a moment, then swung the hat swiftly upward. A little puff of smoke went careening skyward. He did this four times, then put the fire out and rode on. He made no attempt to stay in the shadowy places or near the trees.

While it was still early, he stopped near a ghostly, dark and brooding black-rock canyon and smoked a cigarette, sitting relaxed and patient-looking. He felt nervous, more nervous than he had ever felt before up here. Where were they? Why didn't they come? He nudged his horse out again and kept on going, uneasiness like a whip lashing his spirit.

Between two far peaks — the back door to Soldado's meadow and a perfect ambushing spot — he knew surely the Indians must be watching him. Instinct told him not to go through the narrow gorge. He dismounted and squatted. The sunlight danced off the boulders and lay heavy across his back. He hunkered beside his horse with the appearance of endless patience. It was good acting, for every moment added to his uneasiness.

Then he saw the buck coming toward him. He was slightly taller than the average Apache. His skin lacked a coppery tint, but it was dark. Watching, Will surmised this may have been a captive child raised by the Apaches. Probably originally he had been a Mexican.

Will stood up and waited. The Apache stopped a short way in front of him, with his knees bent a little. His shoulder length black hair was held by a single strip of red cloth perhaps four inches wide. He was possibly a half-head shorter than Will and just as broad, just as deep-chested and heavily muscled. His eyes had a restless, wild look. They were rarely still. He wore the traditional *n'deh b'keh* moccasins with their big toe-buttons. A stubby, scarred, single-shot Cavalry carbine of large bore was carried carelessly in his right fist. In Spanish, speaking slowly, Will asked for Juan Soldado. The Indian turned and told him to follow.

The path was very faint but the Apache followed every twist and curve of it without once looking down. He probably had been over it since early childhood. There was no sound as Will followed the buck, except when the horse's shoes struck a rock now and then. Will had a foreboding tingling.

The guide dipped over the little ledge that went between the sentinel pinnacles, and Will followed, the hair at the nape of his neck standing straight up. Beyond lay the tight little valley where Soldado Creek, with little fall now, puddled outward and made bathing and washing places.

The buck slowed to a shambling walk, and just before he stopped altogether, Will was surrounded by Apaches. They came noiselessly, with an unnerving suddenness, from among the rocks behind the narrow gorge, from the tall grass, from the scattering of trees and shadows.

They stood around him in a silence more ominous than the wildest screams they could have made. It was a bad moment. Their eyes were wet and very dark and as unreadable as the rocks of their stronghold. There was no way to keep fear out of his heart now.

A small, stockily made, moon-faced, broad-shouldered man without an ounce of fat on him came through the throng of men. Will felt the tight ball of his stomach relax a little. It was Juan Soldado, a wispy, powerful Apache with an astringent, hard look. He didn't smile, but he walked up to Will and stared into his face for a moment, then touched him on the chest and spoke in Spanish.

"You are welcome."

That was all. The Indians broke up their ragged circle and began to drift beyond the willow-fringe of the creek where the brush shelters were. The Apache hogans were made in the conical shape of beehives.

Soldado walked away without a glance or a word. Will led his horse and followed. The sweat was running like spilled water under his shirt. He thought that if he came here a hundred times more, it would always be the same.

When they came to the trodden, strong-smelling places of the village, Juan never looked back. Will followed him right up to the door-hole of his brush house, dropped his reins, stooped low and entered. A wizened squaw took his horse away, and he handed her the saddle bag with the fresh trout. A younger squaw hur-

57

ried past him on her way out of the wickiup, face averted, the smell of sage and wild mint following in her wake. She was young and pretty. Will saw that much and no more.

"*Sientesé.*"

Will sat. The weapons and saddles and household goods of the war leader were stacked within the shady place. The air was cool with a strong, musky odor of horse sweat and Indians.

"We saw you coming, Guillermo."

"I didn't think so."

The black eyes, with their muddy whites, swung and fixed themselves on Will's face. "Ah," the Apache said in a reproving way. "You thought you were alone? Unseen?"

"You sent no fighting men to the fishing hole."

"No. I had a sound reason."

"Because you knew me?"

The Apache said nothing for a moment; then he leaned with his hands hanging across his folded knees. "That, yes. Something else too. We are friends. You are our friend — but who knows for how long a man is another man's friend?"

Will looked up, puzzled, but he said nothing.

"You didn't come alone."

Startled, Will's head jerked a little. Juan Soldado's dark eyes showed cold amusement.

"You didn't think we'd know?"

"I came alone — all the way."

"No."

Indignation swept over Will. "Send a man to

58

read my sign," he said. "Follow it all the way back to Melton. I came alone."

Juan Soldado looked at the ground with a tiny frown. "I thought it might be like that, too." He looked at Will swiftly with a probing stare, then rocked a little forward and smiled a cruel smile.

"My guards told me when you came. You were wise in staying close to the mountains, but they watched you after the heat drove you out. They saw you come into the trees and make a camp by the fishing spot."

"Why didn't they come down like they always have before?"

Soldado's smile turned crafty. "I wanted it done this other way," he said. "I thought you were hiding from men, when you rode up here the way you did. Maybe you were being followed." The eyes were blank, black and shiny, waiting.

"It was to keep from being followed that I did that."

"I thought that, too, Guillermo. We are friends."

"I don't understand," Will said. "This is a riddle."

Juan Soldado shook his head. "No riddle. Nothing is strange about it now. There are ten men following your tracks. They have followed you all the way from Melton."

Will knew a kindling of hot anger. "Are you sure?"

Soldado got up swiftly. "Come with me."

They walked back out where the sun was hot. Anger grew in Will's heart. Curtin hadn't kept his promise. Perhaps he shouldn't have expected it, but he had expected it. Common sense should have warned the judge what would happen if he tried to beard the Apaches with ten men. Ten? He watched Soldado's moving back, ahead of him. Counting Mike Allen and the judge, there were only nine in Curtin's party. He thought it unlikely that the judge himself would venture out of the village, but even if he had — who was the tenth man?

One of the Mexicans? Possibly — but not very probable. Grady? Hardly. He was still pondering it when Soldado had crossed the wide meadow where his village lay, scrambled among the jumbled, hot-feeling boulders and stopped low on the edge of nothing, looking downward.

Will grunted up beside him. They stood crouched, with only their heads and shoulders visible. It was an unnecessary precaution but a natural one.

"There. See for yourself, Guillermo."

Down the long vista of heat-bathed desert he saw the horsemen. They were moving slowly. At that rate they wouldn't reach the pass below the fishing hole until late afternoon. He counted them — ten. With knit eyebrows he tried to recognize some of them, and couldn't. He sank down on the hot granite and watched them advance. Juan Soldado, squatting beside him, said nothing. His face was round, shiny, and as hard as rock. He rarely blinked despite the fury of the heat.

"I don't know how they did it, Juan Soldado. I stopped and watched my back trail."

"It wasn't hard. Your tracks are still there for the world to see. They didn't come after you until you were far enough ahead not to be able to see them. They were clever that way — yes. In another way they were very foolish. Only ten of them." He made a knifing motion with his head. "I could send that many young boys to ambush them." He turned and gazed at Will's wooden profile. "Who are they, Guillermo?"

"I think they're men from Melton."

"Ah! But not Mexicans. Then they must be the ones who rode tall in the saddle, beside the buggy. Who are they? What do they want?"

"They're men brought to Melton by a lawman of the settlements, Juan Soldado," Will said slowly, anger making his face savage. He hadn't wanted the mission he was embarked upon to be handled this way. Apaches — like all Indians — were not to be rushed into anything.

"Why are they here?"

"There were some people killed on a stage not far from here — as a bird flies."

"Yes," Soldado said softly, his eyes narrowing. "I know that."

"There were two little boys. They want them."

Juan Soldado swung without speaking and looked after the little band of riders. Will watched them, too. He could tell from the way

61

they rode — slumped, yet determined — that they were doubly dangerous right now.

"And if they don't get the boys, Guillermo — what then?"

Will wasn't fooled by the blandness of the voice. He shrugged, staring at the Curtin riders. "I don't know."

"They will come up here and bring us a fight."

"You don't want that, Juan."

The Indian looked around at him. "No, that's the truth. We don't want them to bring the fighting up here. Here is peace and good living. We've kept it that way." He made a gesture toward the riders. "But they can track you all the way up here. That would mean fighting. We don't want them to go back and tell about our village."

Will stood up and brushed the rock dust off his pants. A feeling of hopelessness swept over him as he straightened up. Juan Soldado turned abruptly and started back. Will followed along. He could see the stir of excitement in the Apaches and caught some of the malevolent looks thrown his way for having led Curtin's crew this close to the hideaway village. It made him angry all over again.

Back at Soldado's brush hut they dropped down in the meagre shade. Will's gaze traveled over the ancient cup of land that lay like a huge saucer behind the upthrusts of granite that ringed it on all sides. Northward lay the pathway he had come over. He cursed Curtin under his breath and his anger crystallized into a slow, steady, resentment against the man.

"They must not come here, Guillermo."

Will nodded. "They will not," he said, looking at his horse, unsaddled, cropping the tough, short grass of the upland meadow. "They won't either, Juan." He shoved up to his feet.

"Can you stop them?" The Indian didn't arise, but his eyes did, swept up to Will's face and lingered there.

"I can try."

"Good. We will watch you at the fishing spot. That will be the best place."

"Yes, they'll want to camp there."

"No, Guillermo. They must not come that far. We will kill every one and their horses as well. It must be this way. You understand it."

"Yes, I know."

"How will you do it?"

"How? I'll tell them to go back."

"Ah! They don't look like the kind of men you can say that to, Guillermo. They are mean-looking. If talk won't work — what then?"

Will's eyes were slitted in thought. "If that won't work I'll let them follow me all over the damned country, Juan, until they drop or I drop."

"That," the Apache said with conviction, "is what it will take. I was waiting for you to say that. I don't like you having to do this. I wish you could stay. We have three wounded warriors and a little girl with a broken toe and some old people

63

who are sick. You are too valuable to us to lose, Guillermo." Juan Soldado reached out and touched Will's chest with his forefinger, very gently. "I won't let you drop."

Will caught his horse, re-saddled, swung up, nodded toward the war leader and rode slowly back down the valley. The heat was over him, on the left side, burning almost as fiercely as his anger was. The Apaches turned from their parapets to watch him go. Softly, from the distance, he heard Juan Soldado call something down by the funnel-shaped entrance. He twisted and looked back. It wasn't meant for him. Apaches were hurrying toward the leader's thatched hut. Will watched a grim moment, then swung forward again and rose down through the narrows.

He knew without glancing up that indignant eyes were watching his progress. It was a bad moment. The sun beyond the gorge was worrying at the monoliths and being repulsed so that the outward flung reflection of heat was very bad. He rode, hardly feeling it.

Judge Curtin was a fool. He was worse than a fool. If he was so eager to get the boys back alive . . . Will cursed aloud.

The slope downward was very gentle. He rode all the way back to the pool, through the sparse pines and firs. Farther down, westering a little, was a trail to the uplands. The riders hadn't reached it yet. At the rate they were going it would be another two hours, anyway.

He longed to stop at the pool but went on by it

with nothing more than a wistful glance. Seeing his own tracks made him resentful. There should be a way for a man to travel so that he left no tracks. He thought of the brick roads in the "States" and shook his head. If such things ever came to Arizona it would stop the white men cold, but not the Apaches. They could read sign where only a hint of it lay or track by scent. He flicked away the sweat and thought wryly, that wouldn't be hard to do in the summertime, when men stank with a peculiar strong odor, like old copper or bronze.

The path had a little of the heat of the desert beyond. He rode through it with his eyes on the rise within the funnel. No riders came into view. He considered waiting there for them, but pushed on. It would be better if they didn't even know the path existed.

Down in the deadly breathlessness of the slot itself, he dismounted, tugged his saddle blanket from under the loose saddle, led his horse out onto the desert and looped the reins around a sumac bush. Then he went back and dragged the blanket very carefully over the soft, spongy earth. When the last track through the funnel was obliterated, he went back, re-saddled, mounted and rode purposefully northward, out onto the desert again.

It was better this way. Better even than letting the trailers know there was such a spot as the fishing hole.

He stopped often and looked back but he

didn't see them coming until the sun was slanted far off its meridian.

From a little hump-backed knoll he watched them for a long time. They were even with the funnel now. Apparently the heat there — his ally for once — kept them from even reconnoitering the pass, for they picked up his new tracks and came forging after him in the grim, sluggish way they were riding.

Then Will hunted shade. He found it on the far lip of an abrupt arroyo where a lonely juniper tree stood. There he dismounted, made himself comfortable under the tree, ate some canned beef and smoked, watching the back trail with an unpleasant, hostile look.

When the Curtin men showed up they were too intent on watching his tracks to see him until they had crossed the arroyo. By then Will had recognized some of them and the leader, gunman Tom Elmore. Antagonism swept over him again. He exhaled smoke without moving, a hard, bitter stare fixed on the sweaty men.

The first rider saw him and made a knife-sharp, sucking sound with his breath. The others looked up quickly. Will's anger was tempered by scorn and ironic amusement. What puzzled him was the fact that neither Curtin or Mike Allen was along. It puzzled him.

Tom Elmore reined ahead of the others. He had his carbine lying across his lap. His heavy face, beef-red and shiny, was oozing oily perspiration. His glance was hot and unfriendly. He waited, but Will didn't move or speak. So he swung down, flexed his legs, and swore. There was no trace of embarrassment or chagrin in the gunman's face.

"You led us quite a chase."

"You weren't supposed to be chasing," Will said slowly.

Elmore's blue eyes went searchingly to Will's face. "No? The judge changed his mind."

"That's too bad," Will said, still more slowly.

"Why?"

"Because now we go back."

Elmore looked thoughtful in a grim way. He held his silence, and Will watched the men dismount, turn their saddle blankets and re-saddle, then stand hip-shot, dog-tired and bone-dry in the small shade of their horses, waiting.

"I don't think we do," Tom Elmore said in a quiet way, each word like a steel ball falling on glass.

Will pushed out his cigarette before he looked up at the gunman again. "Well," he said, "if you're going on alone — go ahead. I'm going back."

"You're going on with us."

Will got up and leaned back against the stringy old trunk and shook his head. "You're wrong, Elmore. You're as wrong as can be. I told Curtin I'd go alone and to keep you fellers out of it. He didn't want it that way so now he can try it his way."

Elmore listened stonily. "Afraid?" he asked.

"Yes," Will said, "afraid of getting the kids killed. And you will if you make the Indians mad."

"Who cares about a mad Indian?"

"I do," Will said. "In this particular case, I do."

Elmore was studying his man. There was a look of blind stubbornness he didn't like. It angered him too. If he couldn't force Will to lead them — then what? A long ride for nothing, a frying, torturous trip back to Melton to report a failure. He swore again, wasting good breath. The curses rained around Will with no apparent effect; at least no visible effect.

"I got an idea I can make you go on, Graham."

Will's anger was just as solid as ever, but up until now it hadn't been directed against Tom Elmore or the other men. They were tools — impersonal beings — to him. Curtin was the treacherous one. His eyes had a smoky look when he spoke now; his lips hardly moved to let the words out.

"That would be the worst mistake you ever made, Elmore."

The gunman's stare froze on Will. "You're fast, eh? How fast?" He moved slowly toward his horse, caught up the reins and began to re-saddle his animal. Elmore watched him in hard silence. Will heard him sigh once just before he mounted and turned his horse and sat there, gazing down at the gunman.

No one said anything. The antagonism,

though, was heavy enough in the shimmering atmosphere to cut with a knife. Will slouched with both hands on the saddlehorn.

"Use your head, Elmore. I won't lead you to them no matter what you do. I'm not even sure I could — now. Another thing — there are ten of you. There might be fifty of them. The third thing — they'll kill those kids."

"Forget the kids."

"All right," Will said softly. "Forget the kids. The rest of it's no less true."

"Graham, ten of us can walk through a whole tribe of those stinkin' devils."

Will regarded the man from the settlements with a sardonic look. "You couldn't walk through an equal number, let alone twice as many. I know."

"You won't lead us, huh?" Elmore seemed to have made up his mind about something.

Will shook his head stonily.

"You'd better think it over, Graham."

There was definite menace in the words now. Will looked at the sweat-drenched gunman, then at his riders. They seemed divided in opinions, if expressions meant anything. He lifted his glance covertly and raked the surrounding brush and rocks with a penetrating stare. He didn't see them but he knew they were there. It put him in a peculiar situation. He had murderous allies the gunmen didn't have any inkling he had — but he didn't want to precipitate a fight either.

"You thought it over?"

He dropped his glance to Elmore's flushed face and steely eyes. "I reckon so."

"Well?"

For answer Will lifted his reins, tugged gently, turned his horse and started riding back down the way toward Melton. For a moment Tom Elmore's glazed face was like fire. His eyes had a wild, awful light in them. Then he swept up his own reins, sprang astride and jerked his head. The watching posse followed after him.

Will swerved and twisted among the spiny brush for a little way, then kicked his horse over into a slow lope and held him to it for a long time. Twice he heard Elmore's shout, and both times he turned, watching the distance more than the pursuit, before he swung forward again and kept on going. It wasn't much of a way out, but it was all he had.

His horse had had rest and water and green feed. He was far fresher than the animals of Curtin's crew. Elmore wouldn't dare shoot him and he knew it. Beyond that he had just the one alternative he was using now: loping, turning, cavorting through the brush with tight shoulders, knowing Elmore's gang wouldn't push their leg-weary, exhausted animals into a run to catch him.

And he was right. Tom didn't chase him. Once he fired his carbine over his head. The song of the bullet told Will that he was still in range. He held his horse to the lope a little longer, hating to do it but doing it nonetheless, until he was well beyond shouting and shooting range. Then he slowed to a fast walk and kept the beast slugging along through the terrible heat until twilight came.

After that he rode by instinct. There was no longer much danger. His horse could stand the gruelling anguish of a night-long ride. The horses of Elmore's men couldn't. They had already been pushed to their utmost.

He kept right on traveling until the coolness told him dawn wasn't far off. Then he reined up and swung down, loosened his cincha, squatted to eat, and listened. There wasn't a sound of any kind until a voice in harsh, unnatural Spanish spoke out of the gloom on his right.

"You are a wise man, Guillermo. Wiser than I thought. You are very shrewd."

He wasn't surprised, exactly, but the sight of Juan Soldado there beside him, motionless, as if he had materialized out of the brooding night itself, made his flesh crawl a little. He went on chewing and looked over at the Apache, saying nothing. Juan Soldado smiled at him. It was a crafty, cruel smile.

"I didn't want a fight, Juan, but I wasn't sure that fool wouldn't shoot me."

"You were taking a good chance."

Will shrugged. "I don't like gambling like that, especially when my back was to him."

"They are in camp behind you. That light-haired one is tough. Maybe I should have him killed."

"And let them know you are around?"

71

"A bullet, Guillermo."

Will shot the Apache a hard look. "That'd be worse. They'd think I did it then."

Juan Soldado considered this for a moment, then inclined his head and shrugged his shoulders. "I tell you this, Guillermo. You may have to do it yet. That man will kill you. You've made a good enemy. You can be proud of having one like him."

Will finished eating, brushed away the crumbs and began to make a cigarette. He offered the sack to Juan Soldado. The Apache took it and very solemnly bent to the task of creating a thin brown quirley of his own. They smoked for a while in silence; then Will blew a long, pale streamer skyward and spoke without looking around at the Indian.

"Let me buy the little boys from you."

The Apache wasn't the least bit surprised. He answered right back, "I don't have them."

"But you know who does have them."

"No. I was south on a raid when that happened, Guillermo."

"You can find out?"

"Yes." Juan looked into the night and cocked his head a little. For a while he said nothing; then he looked down at his cigarette in a thoughtful, wry way.

"Why do you want them, Guillermo?"

"They have an uncle. He wants them."

"But you don't?"

"It's better for the boys' relatives to raise them

than for strangers to do it."

"Apaches?" Juan said softly, glancing up.

"Not necessarily; anyone at all."

"We raise white boys to be great fighters. They make the best Apaches sometimes. If *you* wanted them, Guillermo, it would be different."

"Then I'll take them." It was a fast decision.

Juan smiled thinly. "You wouldn't make a very good mother. You have no woman." Then he chuckled as though he had purposefully led Will up to this. "I'll buy them for you, Guillermo. You come back with me and be an Apache. I'll give them to you for a wedding present. I'll carry your burden to an Apache girl. You'll be an Apache then."

Will looked over his cigarette at the round, smooth face, with its deepening lines and scars. Juan Soldado was still grinning faintly, but Will knew he wasn't altogether joking.

"Juan, I am a far better Apache as I am than I would be if I took the blanket. You'll know that's true if you think it over."

"You're a great medicine man already, Guillermo." Juan stopped there, biting off a breath. He looked into the night past Will and said no more.

Will was relieved that the topic had been closed. He swung back to his original subject. "Will you find out if the boys are still alive?"

"Yes."

"And who has them?"

"Yes."

73

"And how much money he wants for them — or horses — or cattle?"

"Yes, I'll do all those things, Guillermo, but it might take time."

"Fine," Will said grimly. "It will take me time to get back here again, too, Juan. These men will be hard to deceive the second time."

"Ah!" the Apache said in a contemptuous way. "They are fools, Guillermo. You will run around them like coyote." The black eyes held to Will's face with a clear and admiring look.

Will knew the coyote was a symbol to the Apaches; he had heard innumerable coyote stories and legends. It was definitely a compliment to be spoken of in the same breath with a coyote. He snuffed out his cigarette and got to his feet.

"I'll ride the rest of the night, Juan. It will be better for the horse that way."

"I'll go back and take the men away."

Will looked down into the smooth oval face. "You'll find out what I want to know and keep it for me?"

"I said I would."

He left the Indian standing in the hush of the desert and rode over against the high flank of the Galiuros, following the curve south as he had followed it north the day before.

There was the pungency of creosote bush; the metallic odor of parched earth and desert dust. The strange, fleeting scents of desert plants and life, and even, strangely, the perfume of tiny flowers and night-blooming cactus blossoms, made the long ride before dawn enjoyable to man and horse. They clipped off the miles and were back around in front of the Galiuros, towering and pink-tinted with dawn, when the sun finally worked its ponderous, shivering bulk up over the eastern pinnacles again.

Before the heat came, Will found the tracks where Tom Elmore's men had ridden over his trail. Later, when he was soggy with sweat, he found something that solved a puzzle that lay in the back of his mind — fresh horse tracks, more riders going toward Melton. That was it. Judge Curtin had recruits. How he got them, Will had no idea, but he had them. He knew that from the writing on the sand made by shod horses.

He tried to count them. After a while he succeeded, but it was difficult. The horsemen had apparently ridden bunched up, with no stragglers. It made him smile. They were gun-hard, these men from Tucson and the border towns. Hard enough to face each other down and gamble their lives against a fast draw and a sound aim. But this was different. Just the name of Apache was enough to make them bunch up close.

Nine tracks of separate riders. He lifted his squinted glance and watched Melton materialize. Eighteen men, counting Curtin and his camp-striker, Mike Allen. He spat through flat lips and let a disgusted swear word follow. After that he rode without moving, watching the village come closer and closer.

75

Chapter 4

There was no visible life when Will put his horse up in the old Maxwell barn. Even the Mexican dogs weren't on guard for a change; either that or his smell was familiar to them, because none appeared to yammer. He fed his horse well and hiked down to Grady's store. Entering the trading post, he caught the cool, musty odor of the place and called out. Grady came through the door-curtain and blinked at him.

"Didn't expect you back for a week." He stepped aside and held back the curtain. "Come on in; I'm cooking eggs."

Inside, Will dumped his hat in a corner and dropped tiredly onto a slatted chair. "Curtin sent out his riders to trail me."

"I know," Grady said without looking up from the stove. "I saw them go and asked him about it. There wasn't a cussed thing I could do about it."

"Why did he do it? Did he say?"

"Not exactly. I got the impression, though, he doesn't trust you. Why, I've got no idea. He's a devious feller, that judge. Don't know as I've ever seen one quite like him before. And Allen — there's a funny bird. Doesn't say ten words all day long. Sits and stares."

Will listened to Grady's words, his gaze off in

space. There was something wrong here, something off-key. He looked up when Grady put two plates of grease-shiny eggs on the table.

"Why would he do that, Grady?"

The trader's gaze lifted. "Do what? Send those men out?"

"Yes."

Grady poured black coffee and dropped down, frowning. "I don't know. Maybe to get the kids himself. I'll admit it doesn't make sense to me. And I told him he was endangering your life and theirs."

"That didn't bother him, did it?"

"No. Eat up."

Will ate. He didn't speak again until he was finished. "I can't figure it out. He won't get a dime if the kids're killed, and he can't get them without someone to help him, but he endangers everything anyway. It doesn't make sense, Grady."

Grady sucked his teeth thoughtfully. "It's a mystery," he said.

Will heard footsteps in the outer room and glanced over at Grady. The trader was making a cigarette. He got up with an annoyed look and went to the curtained doorway.

"Come on in, Karen."

She entered, and Will was conscious of his disreputable appearance. Her eyes widened a little at sight of him. "Will!"

He arose and pushed out a chair for her. Grady poured a third cup of coffee. She sat looking at Will. Her heavy hair was gathered at the back of her head and held severely by a yellow ribbon. She looked very attractive.

"Did you do it, Will?"

He shook his head. "No, Curtin's men came along. They'd trailed me. I came back."

"I'm glad you're back."

He smiled. "Thanks."

"Well, I didn't mean it exactly like that. I've got something to tell you. That's why I came in early this morning. To tell Grady."

Both men looked at her, slouched in their chairs, waiting.

"I went for a stroll with Mike Allen last night. He told me they had some more men now. Another bunch from Tucson."

"I thought there were more," Grady said shortly. "Seemed to me there was, last night. They keep me jumping, but I'd've swore there were newcomers around."

"There are," Karen said. "I can see their camp from my adobe. There are about eighteen of them over there. That's not counting Mike or Judge Curtin either."

Will made a cigarette and spoke without looking up from it. "I counted their tracks yesterday on the way in. I'd guess them to be eighteen with Curtin and Allen." He lit up and crinkled his eyes at the smoke. "It doesn't make much difference though." He looked steadily at Karen. "What else did Allen say?"

She looked a little flushed but her eyes were

steady. "Nothing much. Asked about you. About Grady. Wondered about Melton and the country around here."

"Did he say anything about Curtin?"

"No." She regarded Will thoughtfully. "You've got something on your mind, haven't you?"

"Curiosity," Will said. He smoked for a moment, then turned to Grady Stewart. "Any idea why he did it?"

"Not a one, Will."

Karen looked from one to the other. She was on the verge of speaking when Will rose, took up his hat and nodded to them.

"See you later."

After he left, Grady and Karen talked. The flow of their conversation was eventually interrupted by the advent of some of Curtin's gunmen. Karen stayed out of sight, cleaning up the dishes while Grady went out front to wait on them.

Will, meanwhile, went in search of Judge Curtin. He found him through the aid of Mike Allen. The fat man was more taciturn than ever. Judge Curtin eyed Will with his iron-hard stare, then motioned him toward a camp stool.

Will stood, looking down at the lean man. "Why'd you send men to follow me?"

"To protect you."

Will's expression grew ironic. "I don't need that," he said. "I don't altogether believe that's the reason, either."

Curtin's face tightened. He drummed on a rickety camp table with his left hand. "Whether you believe it or not, Graham, I don't want anything to disrupt my chances of success in getting the boys back."

Will dropped down on the camp stool and leaned forward a little. "You couldn't have acted with less consideration if you'd tried, Judge. I thought we had that ironed out before I left."

"Reconsideration indicated a wiser course."

Will was silent a moment. His dislike of Judge Curtin was thoroughgoing now. He sighed. "All right. From now on it's in your lap. I'm out of it."

"Where are my men?"

"They'll be along this afternoon or evening. I left them pretty far out."

"Any trouble, Graham?" The grey eyes were like melted iron.

"Not particularly. Just a question of forcing me to lead them to the Indians." Will smiled crookedly. "Your man didn't have much in the way of trading goods, though."

"What do you mean?"

"If he shot me — without orders from you — there'd be trouble. If he had tried to make me lead them, I could have taken them way out and lost them." Will stood up and grinned unpleasantly. "Your Mister Elmore was in a quandary. I imagine he'll tell you about it."

Judge Curtin leaned far back and relaxed in his chair, looking up at Will. "Whether you believe it or not, Graham, that was simply a measure of security for you. You are my sole contact with those savages. I don't want anything to happen to you."

"You mean I *was* your sole contact. Not any more."

"Don't be foolish," Curtin said sharply. "If I have to find the Apaches my way, there'll be a war."

"Sure I know it. What about it?"

"You don't want that. They'll come down on Melton."

"That'd be too bad for you."

Curtin shook his head and smiled a little in a lazy way. "No, not on me. I'd simply move out of Melton and let 'em have it and go some other place and throw up another camp."

Will was nonplussed. The judge was deliberately using the sack of Melton as the price for keeping Will under his control.

"Stewart and the girl, Graham. The Indians'd have a heck of a time telling them from the Mexicans in the dark."

Will's stare was unblinking and a little unbelieving. This was a judge of the bench saying these things, blackmailing him into serving Curtin interests. Offering him Grady's life and Karen's life — not to mention the lives of the unsuspecting Mexicans — for his continued obedience to the Curtin interests.

"I want those boys, Graham. I want them that badly."

Will said nothing. His face was darkly unreadable. He thought of the Curtin gunmen; they were of a border breed. As long as Curtin paid them they'd do exactly what he ordered. If that meant making Melton an Apache target, then pulling out and leaving it, they'd do it. He thought of the fat young man, Mike Allen. He wasn't a gunman. He wasn't Curtin's iron type either. His mind was brought back to the present when Judge Curtin leaned forward toward him, resting his thin arms on the table.

"I don't like to have to use force, Graham, but there it is. Now if I annoyed you by sending out a bodyguard, I'm sorry. The next time I won't. You have my word on it. But you've got to go out and make your contact again. You can leave either tonight or in the morning. Which will it be?"

Will wasn't prepared to answer. He turned on his heel and walked out of the tent without a word. Curtin followed him to the door-flap as though to call him back, but didn't.

Will went back to the post, waded through the crowd of sweating gunmen and went into Grady's room. Karen was sitting at the table with some ledgers. She looked up at him when he dropped down. The dark, flushed look he wore intrigued her.

"What's the matter, Will?"

He considered telling her, then shrugged and looked at the floor. "I just ran into a stone wall," he said. "One of those things like having a cougar by the tail. You daren't hang on and you daren't let go."

"What does that mean?"

"I don't know yet myself."

She could see he wouldn't say any more, so she got up and put the coffee pot on the stove, went back to her books and gazed over at him for a long time in silence.

"Will?"

"Yes."

"It's Judge Curtin, isn't it?"

"Yes."

She was silent for a moment, watching him; then she gave a little rueful smile. "You can be very stubborn when you want to be."

"You're fishing, Karen."

"Maybe I could help," she said.

He looked up at her. There was a sardonic light in his eyes. "Maybe. I don't think so, though. The coffee's boiling."

She laughed softly and went to the stove. While she poured two cups full, he thought. Staring perplexedly at the wall, going back over what Curtin had said. It just didn't ring true. Whether he wanted the Thorndike boys that badly or not, it just didn't sound right. Threatening to arouse the Apaches against Melton, then leave it to be plundered. A judge of the law wouldn't talk like that; wouldn't even think like that. And that talk of sending Elmore out as his bodyguard. That was an out and out lie; he knew it from what Elmore had said.

"The canned cream's gone but there's some beet-sugar left."

83

"Just black," he said, looking into the cup.

"Ready to talk now?" Her eyes were twinkling. "I never saw such a closed-mouthed man before."

"You haven't seen many men," he said, making a face over the coffee. It was too hot and too strong. "Besides, I'm afraid of you, Karen. You get inside a man with your curiosity."

Her smile dwindled. "I couldn't help that, Will, that night." Her tone was gentle and wondering. "Any woman would be curious about you. I'm no different."

He leaned on the table, looking at the steaming coffee. He didn't answer nor move. His mouth had a strong, hard set to it. His blue eyes were unmoving, almost unseeing at that moment. His shoulders were hunched and his face showed tiredness and a brooding worry.

"Why did Judge Curtin send those men after you? Will you talk about that?"

He looked up. "You're the most persistent woman I ever knew."

"Maybe," she paraphrased him, "you haven't known many women."

His look hardened. "I've known enough of them." Then he leaned back and relaxed, looking at her. "You've maneuvered me into a pocket, haven't you? Made me talk about Curtin or women. You're clever, Karen."

She flushed but remained silent, offering him no alternative.

"They trailed me to get at the Apaches."

"But you saw them first."

"No, the Apaches saw them, and I went back and threw them off my trail, then came on back."

Her eyes were wide. "You had already seen the Indians?"

"Yes, but you're the only one that knows it. I'd rather Curtin didn't."

"Oh, they're that close."

"You haven't anything to fear. Melton's in no danger — never has been, Karen. Judge Curtin's responsible for what may happen in the future, but as far as the Apaches are concerned, Melton's safe enough."

"You *know* that, don't you, Will?"

"Yes, I'm not ashamed of knowing Apaches. They're human, too."

"Don't say that," she said. "They're wolves, Will. They've always been out there. I've gone to sleep with that knowledge ever since I was a little girl. I've lived with that idea — that fear."

"But they've never attacked Melton, Karen," he said quietly.

"They might. That's what stays in my head. They might come any night. We'd never know."

"This Curtin and his private army might bring them — yes. Otherwise — no. I'm trying to think of a way to prevent that. Now you know what's bothering me."

"Judge Curtin is strong, though, Will. He has the men and the guns."

"And not a whit of sense to go with them.

He thinks he can ride over the Indians with twenty or so gunmen. He's foolish to believe that."

"Did you and he have an argument?" She was looking straight at him.

It annoyed him, her way of intuitively probing tender spots. "In a way — yes."

"Don't cross him, Will. He has authority."

Piqued, his eyebrows climbed a little. The blue gaze was like agate. "Has he? Not over me, he hasn't."

Her eyes flashed. "You don't question a man's authority when he has twenty guns behind him, Will."

"I do," he said evenly. Her expression showed worry, and he relented a little.

"Karen, Melton's vulnerable to Apache attack. We all know that. If Curtin's mob stirs up a war there'll be the devil to pay. So far they've left the village strictly alone. They have a very good reason for that. If Curtin stirs them up — hunts them up and takes a fight to them — Melton's going to be sacked."

"We've all seen smoke signals on the peaks."

"What of it? The fact is still the same. Melton hasn't been bothered yet. Sure, they're out there. They're just about everywhere, but that doesn't mean anything unless you ask for trouble with 'em. Their signal fires are harmless, Karen. Smoke won't hurt you."

She leaned back in the chair and looked at him. "You think the wisest course is to stay neutral. Is that it?"

"Yes."

"It's a good thing thc other settlements don't feel like that."

He got up swiftly, and his eyes were hot-looking. "The other settlements are either close to Army posts or are large enough to protect themselves. Melton isn't. What good is a dead hero, Karen?" Looking at her, he checked the race of his words and thoughts and drew off inwardly from her. She wasn't going to answer him, he saw that.

He turned and was almost to the curtained doorway before she said anything.

"Will, are you going back to them again?"

"That's what I've been thinking about. I'll go. I've got to go."

"Why?"

"Because I'm afraid of what Curtin's going to do. He'll get you and Grady killed if he keeps on with his present plans."

"What can you do?"

"Try and talk the Apaches into going off on a hunt or something for a while. Get 'em far enough away so Curtin's men can't find them. What else can a man do? You can't reason with Curtin, I've found that out."

"Be careful, Will. They're murderous. Sneaky — that's what I don't like about them So sneaky and quick and sort of ghostly."

He stood hip-shot, looking back at her thoughtfully. "If they didn't live in hiding — if one walked down the middle of the road in Melton — how far would he get?"

"Not far," she said with a trace of grimness. "Don't defend them, Will. With me it's all right, but not around the others." She made a distasteful gesture. "I've heard enough of the things they do."

"Have you ever seen them do those things?"

Her glance lifted swiftly, indignantly. "No, of course not. If I had I wouldn't be here talking to you."

"You might," he said. "You aren't doomed as soon as an Apache sees you, but if you were, you might remember that this was their country first — not ours." He inclined his head. "They didn't fire the first shot, but if they had, it would have been right. We'd do the same. We have done it, in fact, to keep invaders out."

She watched the curtain fall back into place after he was gone. Her glance was sombre and far-seeing.

He shouldered through the throng of men, nodded casually at Grady and went back outside where the quivering heat was nibbling at the stifling shade of the ramada.

Smoking with his legs thrust straight out and his hat tilted low, he whiled away the remainder of the day in the shade of the ramada. Men came and went in a straggling, listless way all afternoon. He watched them from beneath his hat brim. Judge Curtin had gotten together as venomous-looking a gang of cutthroats as he'd ever seen. That was another thing that bothered him. Why hadn't Curtin used soldiers? Granted they were harassed from one end of the Territory to the other. Still, if settlers and freighters could get them, surely a judge could.

He watched the afternoon die. After long breathless hours of hazy, tinted twilight, night-fall came.

He waited until the turbulence of the village died a little; then he sauntered down to the old barn, saddled up and rode out of Melton south-ward, making a big circle around the placc. He had thought over what had to be done, and it didn't include telling Judge Curtin anything. If Curtin meant to keep his word, fine. If he did or didn't, and Will got away undetected, so much the better.

His horse was fresh and brisk. The desert was cooling. He rode all night long with only one stop; at dawn he lay down for an hour's nap. It didn't last much longer than that either. The sun burned him awake.

He pushed on until he was driven away from the Galiuros again; out farther into the desert. The heat had a way of making his thoughts angry. He rode through it with his eyes hidden behind little ridges of flesh, thinking of Judge Curtin's abysmal ignorance.

Twenty or so gunmen in Tucson was a formi-dable force. In Apacheria they wouldn't cast even a small shadow. If a hostile band of even ten Apache raiders found them, the gunmen wouldn't have a chance. One thing to fight in Tucson; another thing to fight coppery foemen they'd never see, from a hundred vantage spots among the boulders. Ten buck-Apaches with their oldest guns were worth fifty of the best gun-slingers from the sink-holes along the border. Killing Apaches was a lot different from shooting drunken cowboys.

By late afternoon he was swinging in toward the funnel pass again. After that it was a little over an hour's journey to the clear-water pool. He made it but his clothing was soggy, his feet slippery in his boots.

Hardly bothering to look around, he dismounted, hobbled his horse and went down by the pool. He lay with his head submerged for long, blissful moments at a time. The trickle of water down the front of his face was heavenly. Then he sat back in a long shadow, made a cigarette, smoked it and looked for the half-dollar he'd thrown into the pool. It wasn't there.

With knowing patience he waited out the sun blast; then, when the heat from the bloody red sun faded, he re-saddled and struck out for the upland meadow where Juan Soldado's people were.

He was almost to it when a voice called softly to him from behind. He stopped and twisted, looking back. The Indian's face wasn't altogether visible. When the man came up abreast of him, he was grinning.

"Water is good over a man's head." He didn't

wait for an answer but strode on by.

Will understood. He followed the buck with a wry look. One could never scc them, but they were always there. For a friend it was a good thing to know. For an enemy . . . ?

Juan Soldado was waiting outside his bush hogan. Will got down stiffly and held the reins out to the old woman. She led the horse away without once looking into the white man's face.

"This time I don't think they'll find you."

"They will if they try hard enough. That's why I rode on in tonight instead of waiting for morning. Better send back some boys to drag blankets over my tracks before sunup."

"Good," Juan Soldado said. "Go inside. There is food there. I'll send the boys."

Will entered the wickiup. There was the young squaw back against the far wall. She was looking very hard at the floor. The ring of Will's spurs seemed to make her muscles quiver. He felt almost as awkward as she did, but very gravely he sat down with his back to her and picked up the bowl of food and began to eat out of it with his fingers.

He was conscious of the young wife's eyes on the back of his neck. It made him uncomfortable.

When Juan Soldado came back he was grinning a little. A black-eyed look shot past Will at the girl was enough. Juan dropped down and the girl scuttled past on her way out. Will caught the delicate scent of sage and wild mint again.

91

Apache perfume. He thought wryly that he had interrupted something.

"The sentinels saw you coming. This time there were none following you." The black eyes probed Will's face approvingly. "I told you they were fools and you were an old grey fox."

"Not exactly," Will said. "I had the word of the man who pays them that they wouldn't follow me again."

"Ah! What good is this man's word? He told you that before, too."

Will finished the bowl of food and set it down, drew out a limp handkerchief and wiped his hands and face. "He is a liar, of course."

Juan Soldado spat something through the opening and spoke with his mouth full. "There are so many liars in the world, Guillermo." He swallowed his food with a bob of his head and squinted his eyes. "I have been thinking of something. I believe I've hit upon a way to make lasting peace."

Will watched him drain off the juice in the bottom of his bowl. There was a raffish glitter in Juan Soldado's eyes. His face was relaxed and pleasant-looking in its moon-like roundness.

"I think what must be done is this: We will put the white men on reservations and pick good Indians to guard them. Then we will pick honest Indians to feed and clothe them, skilled Indians to show them how to hunt buffalo for meat and hide and not kill them by the thousands and leave them to rot. It will take a long time to teach them to live like Indians, old friend. White men are very stupid. We will have to be very patient with them because they are savages." His shoulders rose and fell. His eyes were mockingly grave.

"We must do this, I think, because these white people will destroy everything otherwise. Some day they will destroy themselves, even. They are like the blind rattler, Guillermo. They kill everything, even their own young and themselves. Ahhh! We must be very patient. It will take a long time to civilize them. What do you think of my idea?"

Will laughed. For a moment Juan Soldado stared at him; then he threw back his head and laughed too. It was a good joke. A typical Apache joke; one with a moral to it.

Will nodded solemnly and spoke. "If you wish, I'll go back and tell the white men where to meet — San Carlos Valley, perhaps, on the Apache Reservation. Now that's a beautiful spot — lots of shade and water and plenty of game."

"*Sí, sí,*" Juan Soldado said, going along with it. "And plenty of room too, Guillermo. You must not forget to tell them that. Big country, with lots of room. You can sometimes stretch your arms and not put out someone else's eye — this you must tell them. Only they will not be allowed to stretch so until just before dawn when others are sleeping, or else there would be a lot of one-eyed white people."

Will grinned at the Apache's humor. He suspected that Juan Soldado's high spirits were based on either mescal or Mexican tequila. He had smelt no mescal pits cooking around the encampment, but then, the Apaches didn't usually cook the plant where they lived anyway. It wasn't *tizwin* time, he knew — time of the Big Drunk — but Juan Soldado's usual laconic manner was missing, and his eyes shone with a happy light. Will decided to profit by this unusual demeanor.

"Juan, did you find the little boys?"

"*Seguro*. I told you I would."

"They are alive?"

"Yes. One was sick for a little while. He had the fever. Now he is all right." The black eyes lost a little of their levity and steadied themselves on Will's face. "Tell me, Guillermo. What is there about these two that is so important? Are they a great leader's sons?"

"No, not that I know of. Their father is dead." He frowned at the recollection of Judge Curtin's words: "That's how badly I want them."

Juan reached under his shirt and scratched himself. He was watching Will's face with an unblinking, eaglet stare.

"You are troubled."

"Yes, Juan. Those men who followed me, they are part of an even larger bunch."

"I know. There were more who went to Melton."

"Well," Will said slowly, in Spanish, "I am afraid they are going to try and find Apaches out

94

here. This is bad. We both know that."

Juan's cruel smile flashed. "When we are ready we will let them find us."

"No. That's another thing, Juan. So far this part of the country has been quiet. The Army doesn't think there are Apaches down here. If you ambush these fools they'll send soldiers here. You'll never be able to come back here."

"What can we do? Run from those pigs?"

"Not run," Will said, watching the Apache's face. "Go on a hunt for a couple of months. Go riding into the back country and stay out of sight for a while."

"Ah!" the Apache said softly. "And when we come back from hunting, Guillermo — what then? They will still be here. If they have come to find Apaches they'll stay until they do, won't they?"

"No. If I take the little boys back with me, Juan, they will go away. To make doubly sure that they leave after I take the boys back, you take your people and go a long way off."

"There will be no reason for them to come hunting us then?"

"No."

Juan's shrewd black eyes crinkled up skeptically. "How soon must all this be done?"

"As soon as I can get the little boys back." A premonition swept over Will. He lifted his glance and swung it to the Indian. "Why do you ask?"

"Because I have a war party out. We must be

here when they come back."

"You could send scouts out to find them, to lead them to your new camp."

"Yes, I could do that. What if they have wounded with them, Guillermo?"

Will smiled wanly into the black eyes. Juan Soldado was using the same kind of coercive bartering that Judge Curtin had used. The Apaches considered him a great healer. Juan's soft question was simply a tentative feeler to see if Will would come back to the tribesmen after he had delivered the Thorndike boys.

"I could find you and take care of your sick."

"Good!" Juan Soldado's face split into his crafty smile again. "Tell me — must we do all this right away? Tomorrow?"

"Within a week, Juan. No later." Will relaxed and stretched his legs out in front of him. "Where are the boys? How much must I pay for them?"

"They are here."

Will was startled and showed it. Juan Soldado grinned raffishly.

"You wanted them. You are my brother. I brought them back. Some of Nana's warriors had them."

"What did they cost you?"

"That's a small thing, Guillermo. You have helped me and helped my people. We bought them with horses from all of us. Besides — we stole more horses on the way back home, from some ranchers. I make a present of them to you then."

"Where are they?"

Juan Soldado got up and motioned for Will to follow him. They went out into the starlit night. It was cooler and darker outside the hogan than inside. The moon, what there was of it, was a meagre sliver of milky light in the purple vault overhead.

Will followed Juan Soldado past the dark outlines of brush wickiups and hunkering, silent Apaches. They went out beyond the circlet of hogans where a slightly larger brush shelter was set aside not far from the meanderings of Soldado Creek. There, Juan Soldado stopped and bobbed his head. Will knew the hogan because he had slept there before. It was the "guest house" of the Apaches. No rancheria was ever without one. Slightly larger, a little apart, usually in the most select part of a rancheria, it stood invitingly secluded.

"In there. My wife is with them. Send her back to me. I will see you at sunup."

Will ducked low and entered. The place smelt musty, as though it hadn't been inhabited for a long time. A little stone with part of a guttering candle on it gave out a murky light. Will saw the Apache woman's sloe eyes on him. He spoke to her curtly in Spanish. Without a word she arose and scurried past him.

Alone, he sat down and tossed his hat aside on the horse blankets, picked up the candle and moved it at arm's length until he saw the two small, pale faces peering at him from under motionless bundles of Apache bedding; gaudy Mexican robes and rebozos, and more durable, beautiful, but very dirty Navaho blankets.

"Sit up, boys, let's have a look at you."

They sat up, the younger one very close to his brother. He was a head shorter than the older boy. They were frightened. He could see that the expression was natural to them. Afraid and bewildered too.

"What's your name, son?"

The older boy spoke instantly, as though he had learnt prompt obedience. "Robert Thorndike. I'm twelve years old. This is my brother Sam — he's nine."

"Bob and Sam. Glad to know you. My name's Will Graham." He debated over shaking hands, then leaned far over and extended his arm. The boys both shook his hand. The younger one gave it a hard squeeze and one pump, then huddled round-eyed against Robert again. He hadn't said a word. Will had the impression that he wouldn't, either.

"I don't suppose you ever heard of a town called Melton, have you?"

"No, sir," Robert answered quickly.

"Well, it's across the desert. There's a man there waiting for you."

Robert sat up straighter. The old blankets fell away from his thin chest and shoulders. He was burned almost copper color from the sun. "Is it our uncle? Is it Judge?"

Will blinked at them. "Who?" he asked softly.

"The judge. He's our uncle."

"Your uncle?" He hitched himself a little closer to them and folded his legs under him. "Is your uncle the judge?"

"Yes, he's the judge over at Tucson. Is he the one . . . ?"

"Wait a minute, Bob. Just a second. Let's get this straightened out." Will rummaged for his tobacco sack and went to work with his big-knuckled hands, shaping up a cigarette. When he had it lighted, he looked at Robert again.

"What's your uncle's name, Bob? The judge, I mean."

"Judge Curtin."

"Oh."

It was like a kick in the chest from a fat horse. Judge Curtin their uncle. Then why in the devil hadn't Curtin said so? Why had he told that tall tale about being employed to represent their only remaining relative, who lived in the East somewhere?

Will felt like swearing. Instead, he grunted like an Indian and looked over at the boys again. Their eyes were fastened to his face. He exhaled a grey cloud at the ceiling and smashed out the cigarette with a vicious stab at the packed earth. Why had Curtin lied? Why had he endangered the boys' lives as he had?

"Bob, tell me about your uncle."

The boy seemed surprised. He cast a quick,

darting look at Sam, but there was no encouragement there. Sam had eyes only for the first white man he had seen in months.

"I don't know what to say."

"Well, is he a nice man? Do you like him?"

Robert's bewilderment was very apparent. "Yes, he's nice. He always used to take Sam and me with him when he went buggy-riding summer evenings. And he used to sing frontier songs for us."

"Was he your mother's brother? I mean, was he your uncle from your mother's side of the family?"

"Oh, yes. He'd have to be because our names aren't the same."

"Yes," Will said lamely. "I reckon so. Did he like your daddy, too?"

"Yes, they were brothers, sort of. Especially about the mine."

"Oh. They had a mine together — is that right?"

"Yes, a copper mine. That's what Daddy was looking for this time. Uncle told him about a new place out here. He took all of us with him. It was a bad place to find but we found it."

"Found the place where the copper was?"

"Yes. Sam and I know where it is, too."

Will held his breath for a second, then let it out very slowly. "Bob, is your uncle a little fat man or a tall thin man?"

"He isn't either. He's big and fat. Isn't he, Sam?"

But the only answer from nine-year-old Sam was a bob of his tousled head.

"Big and fat," Will said. "Not tall and skinny, is he, Bob?"

"No, he's taller'n you are and he has a fat stomach. We aren't allowed to say belly."

Then Sam spoke. It was a tiny, frightened voice, thin and high. "He has shaggy hair like the white lion on the book, too."

Will switched his gaze to Sam, but Robert spoke swiftly, explaining, "Sam means like a white lion in a picture book he has. Uncle has a lot of white hair like the lion has."

Will moved over against the wall of the hogan and leaned back on it. He was silent so long the boys squirmed; then he looked over at them thoughtfully and smiled.

"Bed down, boys. We'll take a long, hot ride and you'll need to be strong for it."

"Back to Tucson?"

"Some day we'll go back there. Maybe not tomorrow, but one of these days real soon. Go to sleep now and don't be afraid. I'm going outside but I'll be back."

He waited until the two heads were almost hidden under the old bedding; then he ducked out through the door-hole, walked slowly over where the high ramparts were, and sat down heavily.

So Judge Curtin wasn't Judge Curtin. Who was he?

Chapter 5

At sunup Will watched the Thorndike boys
crawl out of their mound of old bedding, duti-
fully fold it, stack it away against the brush wall
and stand uncertainly looking down at him. He
hadn't undressed except for his boots and hat.
Now he lay there gazing at them with his arms
folded under his head.

"Do they feed you, boys?"

"Yes," Robert said, "we eat with Juan
Soldado."

Will sat up and smiled. Robert would be a tall
man some day. He was lanky and stringy. His
ribs showed painfully right now. Little Sam was
blockier. He'd be broad and very strong. The
Apaches liked his kind. They made top-notch
fighters out of them. But with Sam, Will could
see, they'd never succeed too well. There was a
soft, doe-like gentleness in his eyes.

"Better go out and splash up. I'll go up to Juan
Soldado's and see when we eat."

As soon as they left he finished dressing, got
up and strolled outside. The morning was cool,
degrees cooler than it would be down on the
desert floor. He saw Indians heading for the
creek bank. He went over himself, scrubbed with
yucca soap and sand, combed his hair with

crooked fingers, then went over to Juan Soldado's hogan.

The chieftain greeted him with a pleasant Spanish salutation, then looked past him. Interpreting the look, Will dropped down beside the Apache before he spoke. "I sent them to wash up."

"I'll send for them." He sent the young wife. The older wife looked at Will with unabashed directness and said something to her husband in their native tongue. Juan laughed and made no answer. Will ignored it, knowing the Indian sense of humor as he did.

"Do they look all right to you, Guillermo?"

"Yes, a little thin perhaps."

"Ah! That's those Tontos. They never have enough to eat." Juan watched the boys trailing diffidently behind the young squaw. Will watched too. They looked perpetually frightened. Sam hugged close to his taller brother, and Robert kept his head high but with an effort.

"Juan, I want you to do me a couple of favors."

"What, then?"

"I'm going to write a letter on paper. I want you to send a man to Tucson with it." He looked at the Apache. "It will be dangerous."

"No, not dangerous especially, Guillermo. Most of my warriors have been in and out of Tucson this past year. We have a lot of Navaho clothing and blankets. The white men can't tell one Indian from another. An Apache hangs thirty pounds of Navaho turquoise on himself, wears Navaho clothes and they think he's a Navaho. What does he do with this letter?"

"He should look for a man named Judge Curtin and give it to him. If he can't find Curtin, he's to give it to the sheriff. Can that be done?"

"Easier than stealing American horses, Guillermo," Juan said. "What is the other favor?"

"I want you to keep the boys with you for a little while longer." Juan Soldado blinked his beady eyes but didn't speak. The old squaw set food before them as the boys came up and dropped down Indian fashion, stony-faced and silent. Will turned to Robert and spoke in Spanish. The boy looked as if he wanted to understand but couldn't.

"We don't know much of that," he said in English. "We're learning though."

"I'll bet you are," Will answered. He turned back to Juan Soldado again and spoke in Spanish. "Juan, there's something going on about these boys that I don't understand."

"Do you mean among the white people?"

"Yes."

"I'm not surprised," Juan said tartly, fishing in his bowl with the first two fingers of his right hand. "White people are tricky."

"Some of them sure are," Will said. "I want to leave the boys here until I ferret out a little of this mystery. Maybe for a week or so. I'll give you money."

Juan shook his head without looking up.

"Money! Guillermo, I've got seven sacks of that buried in the stronghold. Of what good is it? It doesn't heal wounds or feed horses or men."

"All right, I'll bring you back some horses when I come again."

"Mules, Guillermo. Bring me three fat mules. Horses are good to ride, better than mules, but mules are the best eating." Juan Soldado looked up at Will suddenly. "We'll take the boys with us."

"You've decided to go hunting?"

"There was a council after you went out last night. The people think like you do, that we should go away for a while."

"I'm glad of that."

After they had eaten Will took the boys over by the craggy ramparts where there was a meagre kind of shade, and sat down with them. He didn't look into either face when he told them they wouldn't be leaving the Indians just yet. He knew intuitively that Sam's chin was quivering and that Robert's face had paled and his eyes looked stricken.

"For your own safety, boys, it's got to be this way. That doesn't make sense to you, I know, but it's true, I'm afraid."

He allowed them enough time to hide their hurt again; then he looked over at them and smiled. "I'm sorry, as sorry as you are, but right now I think you're safer with Juan Soldado than you'd be with me, or in Melton either, for that matter." He reached out and put a hand on each of their shoulders, squeezed a little and rocked them. "I'll be back for you as soon as I can. The Indians are going to leave here and go hunting. You'll go with them."

"How will you find us?" Robert blurted out.

"It won't be hard. I know Juan Soldado very well. I'll talk to him before I leave." He withdrew his hands and got up, gazing down at them. "Do what they tell you and learn about them. Some day you'll forget the hardness of it and look back on your stay with Juan Soldado's Apaches with a lot of pride. They aren't as terrible as the newspapers make them. They're human — remember that."

He left the boys, went back to Juan's hogan, rummaged inside a saddlebag, and found some wisps of paper. Dredging out a broken pencil from a far depth of the leather pocket, he sat down to write a cramped letter.

Juan Soldado came out and sat down beside Will. With unconscious aplomb he leaned far over and watched the words uncoil from the tip of the pencil. When Will folded the thing carefully, Juan Soldado took it, held it for a moment as though to weigh it, then got up and walked out where the men were herding in the loose horses.

Will waited until Juan returned before he caught his own horse, saddled him and swung up. The heat was beginning to bear down. Juan Soldado came over and squinted up at him.

"We will go to the Apache fork of the San Pedro, Guillermo. Back in where there are some cliffs and caves the Old Ones used."

"If I follow Apache fork I'll find your new camp?"

"Yes."

Will leaned over and extended his hand. "Adios."

The Indian pumped his fist, stepped back and made a fluid, slithering motion with his arm through the air. "Adios," he said.

Will rode as far as the fishing hole, dismounted there and bathed, then pushed on down-land and through the funnel pass and out onto the desert. The heat beat against him. He was mindful of it, but as an annoyance to be borne. His mind was on other things.

A feeling of very real danger was in him. Not so much for himself as for the village and the Thorndike boys. The man who called himself Judge Curtin was up to some scheme that obviously wouldn't stand for any interference or delay. He hadn't thought Curtin cared much about the boys' welfare from the day he discovered that Elmore's gunmen were trailing him. Now he was certain of that.

Curtin's veiled threat about Melton was an even better indication of how the man's mind worked, and whatever happened now, Will would have to be extremely careful. The boys were as safe as he could make them, so his remaining chore was simply a matter of stalling Curtin and his gunmen. That was all he had to do.

The day spun itself out and so did the night. He rested twice, for an hour each time; then, before dawn, he was back in Melton. After putting up his horse he went down to Grady's trading post and knocked with his fingers over the locked door. Stewart, like all men who slept with one eye open and one foot on the floor, was aroused easily. He admitted Will with a dolorous wag of his tousled head and led the way to his living quarters. There, he groped for a lantern, but Will stopped him.

"Don't bother with that thing, Grady. I like the dark right now."

Grady knuckled his puffy eyes and dropped down on his cot, feeling for his trousers. "Well, did Curtin's hounds follow you again?"

"No, not that I know of. Anyway, I found the boys. They're both all right. A little scairt maybe. A little thin. Juan Soldado's going to keep them for me for a while."

"Juan Soldado! Do you know that old devil?"

Will nodded, dryly amused by the explosive way Grady Stewart said the Apache's name. "Yeah, Juan's a good hombre."

The trader snorted derisively. He puckered up his eyebrows. "Why didn't you fetch the boys back?"

"It's a long story. I'll tell you about it later. Right now I want you to tell me everything you can think of about Judge Curtin."

Grady combed his hair with his fingers. He was looking from beneath shaggy eyebrows with a puzzled expression; a searching, perplexed, look. "I don't know any more than you do. Maybe less. He doesn't talk much. Comes in here maybe once a day. Usually, this Mike Allen runs his errands. What about him?"

"What's Allen say about him?"

"Nothing. What the devil — Allen's his right hand man. You wouldn't expect Allen to say anything about his boss, would you? What's on your mind, Will?"

"Curtin," Will said, tartly. Then he got up, crossed the room to a built-in wall bunk, kicked off his boots, tossed aside his hat and flung himself down on it. "Judge Curtin, Grady. There's something awfully wrong with him."

He went to sleep with Grady Stewart's gaze resting on his beard-stubbled face. He slept until long after sunup and wouldn't have awakened then except that Grady was shaking his shoulder with a baffled, worried look. The sounds from the big room beyond indicated that a few of Curtin's gunmen were congregating already.

"Wake up, Will."

"What is it? What's wrong?" He sat up with a start, his heart slugging painfully in his chest.

Grady was scowling. "Maybe I'm wrong, Will. Probably am, but Curtin's sent out almost all his crew."

Thoroughly aroused, Will grabbed at his boots and tugged them on before he stood up. "Where are they going?"

"I don't know, only I've been piecing things

together and've come up with the possibility that Curtin's smarter'n we've given him credit for being. Listen — he couldn't track you when you went out. He knows that — found it out the time he tried it — so he let you go. Now, somehow, he knows you're back."

"And he's sent men to back-track me," Will concluded for Grady with an abrupt curse.

"Maybe I'm wrong, but I figured you should be told anyway."

"I don't think you're wrong, Grady." Will thought it not only very likely, in view of what he already knew about Curtin, but it also made him aware of just how thorough Curtin was. He had sentries out too, otherwise he wouldn't have known that Will was back. Sentries who had either seen him ride into town before dawn, or who patroled the old Maxwell barn and found his horse.

"How many men did he send, Grady?"

"Darned if I know. Looked to me like about fifteen or so. Anyway, there aren't many outside now. Just Allen and a few others." The trader was worried. "You said you left those kids with Juan Soldado. Will, if Curtin's buckos find the Indians, take a fight to 'em."

"That's not going to happen, Grady."

"They won't find the Indians?"

"No. Curtin's plenty smart. Right up to now I've underestimated him. But his own ignorance is what's going to beat him this time."

"What do you mean? Will, your tracks'll be

clear as crystal for a lot longer'n they'll need 'em to travel by."

"Sure. Like I just said, Curtin's smart but he doesn't know Apaches. They have sentinels on the peaks. They'll see Curtin's boys before they get ten miles out. It won't take Juan Soldado long to figure what they're doing. He'll have all day to watch them."

"So?"

"So he'll send out warriors who'll drag blankets over my tracks to obliterate them; then he'll send a decoy to lead Curtin's crew all over the desert."

"Are you sure? Will, if there's a fight . . ."

"They won't kill the kids anyway, Grady. Not now. Not when Juan Soldado knows I want them alive. We're friends, old-timer. Maybe that doesn't mean much to you, but to an Apache it means a lot."

They stood in silence for a while; then Grady Stewart ripped out a tart oath. "What's the mystery around this Judge Curtin, Will?"

Will looked at him thoughtfully for a moment. "Not for publication, Grady."

"Of course not." Grady showed quick irritation.

"To start with, he's not Judge Curtin. I talked to the Thorndike boys. They described their uncle — who is Judge Curtin — and our judge isn't the same man at all!"

Grady looked briefly startled; then he made a short, unpleasant laugh. "It's the darnedest country. Makes a man as dishonest as it is," he said. Then he fisted his hands and rammed them deep in his pockets and looked disagreeable in a sulky way. "What the devil's it all about?"

"I'm trying to find out, Grady. That's why I came back this time. That's also why I asked you what you knew about Curtin when I pulled in this morning."

"Oh." Grady's dour contemplation of Will's face continued. "I've got an idea, Will. This Mike Allen — the fat man — he's been walking Karen every evening. Maybe she's ferreted something out of him about the judge. Knowin' her, I'd say she's tried by now."

Will smiled slowly, remembering Karen's curiosity about him. "I'll go see her."

He did, and caught her just as she was eating breakfast. He was invited into her little adobe house to eat with her, and started digging for information without any preliminaries.

"How're you and Mister Allen making out?"

She shot him a surprised look which he avoided by the simple expedient of stirring his coffee.

"Making out? What do you mean, Will?"

He laid aside the spoon and smiled at her. "What've you found out about Curtin? You've been mining for information. I'd bet on that."

The girl flushed. Her eyes had a steely flash and she didn't answer right away.

"I'm not being facetious, Karen, honest."

She lifted her gaze and stared straight at him.

Her cheeks shone from a brisk scrubbing and her eyes were as clear as a desert sunrise. An uncomfortable warmth spread through him. He was blushing without being aware of it. She looked away quickly when she sat down across from him.

"Mike doesn't talk about Judge Curtin very much. I don't think he likes him. It's in little things he says."

"Like what, exactly?"

She nodded at his plate. "Those eggs'll get cold."

He started to eat. There was impatience in every stab of the fork.

"For one thing, Mike said the judge is a brutal man. Another time he said he'd be very glad when they could leave Melton."

"What else?"

"That's about all. He's very reticent."

"But he likes your company."

"Is that a crime?" she shot right back at him. The steely look was more pronounced.

"No," Will said slowly. "Not at all. I do too."

"You don't show it."

He finished the eggs and leaned back, looking at her. "I didn't know I liked it, until that night we sat on the steps of the church."

"Well, you've been here almost two years now."

He nodded, saying nothing, just looking at her, watching the color mount warmly under her skin. "Could you do something for me? I'm trying to find out a few things about Curtin. Could you get Allen to talk and let me know what he says?"

"He doesn't say much about the judge. I told you that."

"He might if you dug a little, Karen. You've got the knack, you know."

Her anger came back swiftly. She looked at him in a long moment of indignant silence, then spoke. "Maybe it isn't curiosity, Will. Maybe . . ."

"Yes?"

"Nothing." She finished her coffee, put the cup down harder than she had to and started to get up.

"Karen, why are women curious?"

She settled back in the chair. "Because they're interested. I told you that the night on the church steps. I don't care about Mike Allen and the judge. Mike, it seems to me, is afraid of something. It might be the judge. I rather think it is. If he wasn't afraid of him, why would he stay with him when he dislikes him?"

"That's good reasoning," Will said. "Go on."

"The judge is here to get those Thorndike boys. His temperament is wrong for a job like that. Grady and I talked about that the time he sent men to track you. He knows nothing about Apaches. He imagines he can force them to give up their prisoners. His methods seem to be based on force. Maybe that's because of his legal standing."

"Maybe," Will said softly.

Misunderstanding, Karen frowned a little at him. "You asked what I thought and that's it. I'm interested in Judge Curtin for the reason that he's here, and for no other reason. The same applies to Mike Allen."

"Doesn't the judge come around to talk?"

"Not to me. I don't think he cares about women. Another thing, Will, I think he's given orders that his gunmen aren't to talk to me either."

"How about Mike Allen?"

"No," she said slowly, "I don't think he's forbidden Mike to come calling. But the others avoid me like I had the measles."

"Mike's an exception. I wonder why?"

She smiled impishly. "Do you? I think it's because Mike's as interested in you as you are in Judge Curtin."

Will digested this without blinking. "How do you mean?"

"He asks a lot of questions about you. Where you came from, how long you've been in Melton, what kind of a man you are — things like that."

Will's eyes had an intent, shrewd look. "That so?" he said quietly. "I'm glad to know that." He got up. "Thanks for the breakfast. Maybe we could go for a walk sometime. You reckon we could?"

"I reckon."

He left her after that. Outside, the sun was savagely at work fluffing up the roadway dust and hurling wave after wave of molten heat against the adobes. He walked over to the old barn, watered his horse, forked him another big bait of loose hay, then stood back in the shadows of the sagging overhang and made a cigarette.

Melton was almost like a ghost town. Only an occasional distant sound of human activity came to him. Mostly those were from the Mexican *Jacals*. The desert did its shimmering dance of death in the distance. His ribs were damp and sweaty. There was a saturnine look on his face as he gazed from beneath his hat brim out where Curtin's trackers would be by now. It amused him to think how they'd be sweating, cursing, and suffering through the torturous maze of thorny brush and merciless heat, following tracks that the Apaches would have altered to suit themselves.

There was grim pleasure in the thought that Curtin's men would soon be involved in the same project Will was concerned with. The dangers of the land and the motives of the men in it were unfolding. It was a matter now of staying alive.

He stomped out the cigarette and turned to go back into the barn when he saw Judge Curtin and Mike Allen coming toward him. He studied them both, noticing Allen's shuffling, hang-dog look and Curtin's brisk manner that was in contrast to that of the other man. He waited for them to come into the shade.

"Glad you're back," Curtin said. There was a speculative gleam in the background of his small, blue-grey eyes that never moved, once his glance was fixed on Will's face.

"So am I," Will said thinly. "Pretty hot out there."

"Did you find out where the boys are?"

Will looked casually at Mike Allen. The fat man's youngish face was hung with trailing chins that disappeared beneath a limp collar.

"Yes, I found out where they were."

Curtin's eyes moved then, brusquely, appraisingly. "Fine, splendid. Now how do we get them back?"

"It'll take about a dozen fat mules to ransom them," he said, knowing there were no mules closer than Tucson.

"Mules," Curtin said. "How about giving them the money to buy the mules with?"

Will looked a little disgusted. "Who'd sell an Apache a mule now?"

Curtin nodded. "Money wouldn't move them — is that it?"

"That's it. Money's no more to Apaches than air is to us."

Curtin turned his head and stared at Mike Allen. "You could take the boys and go to Tucson and fetch back some mules, couldn't you, Mike?"

Allen nodded apathetically. He neither spoke nor looked at the judge. Will watched them both. He got the impression that this had been said for his benefit; that Curtin had no intention of sending for mules and Mike Allen knew it. He shifted his stance and stood hip-shot, waiting. Apparently Curtin wasn't going to say anything about the men he'd already sent out to find the Indians.

The marble-like eyes came back to Will in an inquiring way. "There's no other way to get the boys back, eh?"

Will shrugged, considered his answer thoughtfully, then spoke. "There might be, Judge. They might take horses. I didn't try to barter with 'em. I asked and they said mules. I let it go at that because I was primarily interested in finding the boys right then, not bringing them back."

"I see. How many're in this band that has them?"

"Bucks? Fighting men? Oh, possibly eighty," Will exaggerated blandly.

Mike Allen's head shot up at that. He threw a daggered look at Curtin.

The judge seemed impressed but not worried. "Eighty. They don't usually have that many warriors, I've been told."

"Your information about Indians," Will said in a dry tone, "isn't very accurate anyway, Judge. Not from what I've heard you say."

Curtin was stung a little. It was obvious, though, that he was too engrossed with other thoughts to be more than passably angered. "No? Possibly not. I know this much from the record, however. Apaches are easily routed in

118

combat. They won't fight a pitched battle."

Will looked out over the desert again. His answer was drawled. "They don't like to fight a pitched battle, Judge. Let's put it that way. They're trained ambushers. There are none better. In their own country — fighting as they've always fought — there's no one who can equal them. They've outfought the Army a hundred times and still will, but you're overlooking something. They're seldom able to muster man for man with the Army. If they're even in numbers, they'll fight without hiding or falling back." Will brought his glance back and hung it on Curtin's tight-skinned face.

"Let's say you were to send out fifteen men or so hunting Apaches. They'd either kill every one of them or lead them such a wild goose chase — if your men were following tracks, for instance — that they'd probably die way out in the desert — and never even see an Apache."

That time Mike Allen swore. The words had feeling in them. Curtin, though, was looking at Will with a cold regard. His eyes were squinted a little although he were in the shade. He canted his head to one side.

"Graham, are you telling me this will happen to men I might send out?"

"Are you considering sending any out?" Will countered.

The judge's head stayed sideways and his stare was like agate. "Let's stop fencing. You saw them go."

Will shrugged. "The thing that matters is that they're gone, Judge. It was a fool thing to do. I've told you that before. Oh, the reason and the way you did it was plenty smart; just the stupidity that led you to send them out is dangerous. Just like the time you tried trailing me. I told you then you'd endanger everything by doing it. Tell me something, Judge: why the devil can't you be patient? I'll get the boys back. It'll take time but I'll do it. Why don't you be sensible and wait?"

"I told you before, Graham, that I'm in a hurry to wind this up."

"All right, but haste here means failure."

"You mean the Apaches'll lead my men astray on the desert?"

"Yes."

Curtin threw his gaze out over Melton's hovels and down toward Grady's trading post. He flicked a contemptuous glance at Mike Allen, who avoided his look and stared morosely at the desert. He looked back at Will, his eyes steely. His voice was flat and solid, like the sound of a fallen tree when it strikes the ground.

"Graham, saddle up and go out there; find my men and bring them back. Then go get those two kids and fetch them back with you. I don't give a darn what you have to promise the Indians. *Get those kids!*"

Will was wooden-faced and motionless. He read the hardness of Curtin's stare correctly and waited.

"I'll give you the alternative — Melton. The

Apaches can't wreck it any better'n I can, Graham."

Will's anger was intense. He couldn't keep it from his eyes and didn't try. "Not with just you and Allen, Curtin."

"We aren't alone. There are still enough of the boys around to help." Curtin bit off each word.

Grady and Karen and the unsuspecting Mexicans. He speculated on his chances right then of tackling Curtin and Mike Allen. Of the latter man he had no doubts. Curtin was something else again. He looked past the pair of them and saw three men standing up under Grady's ramada, looking down toward the barn, watching. It made him feel like cursing. Of course if Curtin was smart enough to think up a way of back-tracking him then he was also smart enough to set up this present situation so that resistance on Will's part would be a signal for the sack of Melton. Very clever. Grady would not know what was coming until it hit him. Karen too.

"Well, spit or close the window!"

Will looked back at the lean face and loathed it. He felt respect, though, for Curtin's ability. In the back of his mind was the knowledge too, that Curtin, however clever he was in many ways, was abysmally ignorant of Indians. Somehow Will could use that against him. It was the only weapon he had left.

"If you're going, Graham, you'd better get started. The boys have half a day's start on you already."

Will drew in a deep breath and exhaled it. He turned and stalked into the barn and began to saddle up. Curtin and Mike Allen moved as far as the doorway, watching him. None of them spoke until Will was mounted and kneeing his horse through the doorless opening; then Curtin's death's-head grin was like creases in wet, dark leather.

"You're pretty savvy at that, Graham. I had another approach but I won't have to use that now."

Will gazed down at him. "What was it?"

"You. I've been gathering information about you ever since we've been here."

"Come up with anything?" Will asked quietly, a glint of interest in his face.

"Enough. You showed up like an outlaw here. Rode in one day and been here ever since. Close-mouthed, do a lot of riding — it adds up to outlaw."

Will smiled broadly. "You're smarter than I thought you were, Judge."

Curtin's eyes narrowed. "I'll get by," he said. Then he hesitated before he spoke again. "And when you get back, Graham, don't run off. I think you and I can get along well enough. We haven't this time, but that don't mean anything. This is a big country. There's plenty in it for two like us."

"What's that mean?"

Curtin shrugged, nodded at Mike Allen and started back uptown toward the trading post.

The ring of his vicious little spur rowels made a plaintive sound.

Will rode down through the village without glancing either way. Some scrawny Mexican chickens scurried ahead of his horse, making foolish cries of alarm. The dust rose in little puffs under the horse's hooves and the heat curled around man and beast with cloying hunger.

He knew the judge, Mike Allen, and the Curtin riders who were still in Melton were watching him from the ramada of the trading post. It made his shoulder muscles crawl a little.

Curtin was a killer. Mike Allen was some kind of a weak fool who was intimidated by the judge. He'd felt that back at the barn. The gunmen Curtin had imported were wolves and nothing more. All the evil and danger was concentrated in the judge. The others were tools.

He had no doubt at all that Curtin would turn Melton inside out, exactly as he had said. He made a cigarette and smoked it thoughtfully. There was still the delaying to be done. That was the main reason he'd taken this alternative and agreed tacitly to ride out and fetch back Curtin's crew. Melton, Karen, Grady, and the totally ignorant Mexicans were also a major consideration, but his two prime motives now were to delay Curtin's plans as much as he could — in the face of Curtin's furious hurry and also the matter of staying alive.

If he could accomplish both and weave his

own warp of subterfuge carefully enough, he might save Melton, the Thorndike boys, Grady and Karen and possibly find out what the entire affair was all about.

Chapter 6

The tracks went as straight as an arrow toward the bony flanks of the Galiuros. He followed them and guessed at the freshness of the horses and men from the way they traveled. After he had swung northwest to skirt the shimmering rock, the tracks became less direct, more sluggish, as though the heat had struck the gunmen about where the mountains curved.

He kept his course until he could see the funnel pass into Juan Soldado's upland rancheria; there the tracks moved out, away from the rejected heat off the towering rocky eminence and farther westward into the desert. He smiled. His anxiety over the Apaches' skill at obliterating his tracks and substituting their own misleading ones had never been too great, but he'd worried a little about it nevertheless. Now, though, he saw how the gunmen were being led farther west all the time. And while he never found the decoy tracks, he knew what Elmore was following.

The daylight hours waned and when he thought dusk must catch him a long way from water or Curtin's crew, he sought out a shale hillside and worked his way up it. Squatting under the fierce heat, he swung his head slowly and studied the land to the west.

It was a long wait but he saw them: small dark objects wandering aimlessly; a large group of riders that had lost its original cohesiveness; gunmen at the mercy of the desert, the heat and the Apaches. He imagined how the Indians would be smirking bleakly over this, and got up. Thirst was a very real torment. He gazed longingly toward the funnel that led to the fishing spot, gauging his distance carefully, knowing he'd have to make it back to this spot before the sun came up again, or never make it.

His horse was caked with salt-sweat crystals when he reined him around on the tracks of the Curtin men again, but the sun was fast sinking now. When twilight came both Will and the animal felt relieved. They kept up their slow pacing over the hardly discernible tracks until he smelt smoke; then the horse pricked up his ears and Will knew the time had come to meet Curtin's killers.

When he came into their camp he saw the discouraged look of the men. They all turned and gazed at him apathetically, and Tom Elmore was the only one who showed any interest. The others were red-eyed, with cracked lips, looking deadly as rattlers but sunk in inertia.

"What you doin' out here, Graham?"

Will felt, rather than saw, Elmore's quickening resentment. He swung stiffly down and stood beside his horse looking at the gunman. "Curtin sent me out to bring you boys back to Melton."

"What for?" There was frank dislike in Elmore's face.

"Because the Apaches outsmarted him, that's why." Will knelt and drew his reins slowly through his fingers. "You think you're back-tracking me. You aren't. You're following an Indian's tracks. He's deliberately leading you so far out you'll never get back. For a while I thought he might lead you in a big circle and leave you back in front of Melton. I don't think that now — not the way he's taking you. One more day like this one — the way you're going — and you won't be able to get back."

The gunmen were watching him with haggard looks. Tom Elmore hadn't moved since Will rode into the dry-camp; now he let out a loud sigh and rubbed a sleeve over his peeling, shiny face. He swore sulphurously for a moment before he let his arm drop, his shoulders droop, and turned off the venom.

"You're smart, aren't you, Graham? You set them Injuns to this, didn't you? I got a notion to spread-eagle you out here and let the sun burn your cussed eyes out. How'd you like that?"

"You're talking like a fool," Will said. "How'd you get back?"

"Get back?" Elmore looked more scornful than doubtful. "Oh, we could find our way back easy enough. We can track ourselves." Elmore's eyes were bright and glittering with rancor. He turned toward a thin, slash-mouthed youth who was tall and sickly-

127

looking. "George, take his gun."

Will stood up as the gunman named George shrugged to his feet and started toward him. "Hold it, mister." He looked at Elmore again. "You *are* a fool. Listen; your tracks aren't behind you any more."

"Darn you, Graham," Elmore said with sudden understanding. "You're playing the Apache game too, aren't you? Brushed out our tracks so's we couldn't get back."

"I didn't," Will said. "I didn't have the time even if I'd wanted to. Elmore, you're like Curtin. You don't know Apaches. Don't know Indians at all, in fact. That's the trouble with you town gunmen. You think a fast draw's all that counts in Arizona. You're wrong. The Indians are ambushing you without firing a shot. They'll lead you so far into the desert you'll all die before you can get halfway back. They'll brush out your back-tracks, too. That'll complete their strategy. You'll be lost. You're lost right now. You've got just one chance of getting out of this alive. Me."

The cadaverous young gunman looked quickly at Tom Elmore. There was agreement in his voice when he spoke. "He's right, Tom. If them Injuns drug blankets over our tracks we'd be lost surer'n hell. He knows this country; we don't."

Elmore's face was scarlet. His eyes were murderous. He didn't speak at all. Will waited until the gunman had turned away to rummage in a saddlebag for food; then he squatted again. An older gunman, with whiskey-puffed features and a bluish tint under his pouched eyes, gazed calmly at Will.

"One man ag'in' fifteen an' you made 'em come to law. Awright, mister, you win — get us out o' here."

"That's why I'm here," Will said crisply. "You'll have to mount up right now though. You can't waste any time. We've got to be clear of the Galiuros before sunup."

"That means all night ridin', don't it?"

Will nodded and swung into the saddle, looked down at the gunmen and waited. They growled among themselves. They were all exhausted, stiff and suffering. Tom Elmore turned back and regarded Will with dry-eyed hostility while he chewed and said nothing. He didn't have to speak; the look was enough.

Will watched them re-saddle and mount their gaunt animals. He turned before the last of them was ready and started down the land. The gunmen followed him in a shambling way, their baleful eyes bloodshot and swollen. Somewhere in the night a little desert owl made its lonely, eerie cry. Will smiled at the sound and two of Curtin's men cursed. The imitation was perfect. Under any other circumstances they might have believed it was an owl. Now they all knew better. There were Apaches out there somewhere.

Curtin's men bunched up their horses a little. The smell of sweat was strong in the heavy air.

Will didn't look back nor ride with any of the others. They left him alone and he returned their coolness. Pushing himself and his horse hard, he kept to the trail until Tom Elmore cried out for his men to stop. The command was dripping with indignation and wasn't meant to include Will, but he stopped also, wheeled and gazed at the nearly worn-out riders. The grim pleasure he derived from their suffering didn't show in the night. Elmore walked his low-headed horse up beside Will and looked challengingly at the guide.

"What's the sense o' goin' on until you drop, Graham?"

"I told you back there we had to get away from the Galiuros before sunup. It's twice as hot against the mountain as it is out on the desert."

"How much farther before we're in the clear?"

"Long way. Maybe fifteen miles."

"We can make it by dawn."

For answer Will lowered his head significantly and looked at Elmore's spent horse. His meaning was perfectly clear without amplification. The gunman shot a glance at his mount, then swore.

"What of it? They've only got to last to Melton."

"They won't, though, unless you use your head."

Elmore leaned a little in his saddle. "You've been ridin' me for a long time, Graham. Been spoilin' for trouble." He straightened up. "All right. You'll get it. Soon's we're in the clear, by God, you'll get it!"

Will dismounted without comment, swung his horse so it cut off his view of Tom Elmore, and loosened the cincha. He made a cigarette and smoked it. It tasted like tar and the dryness of his parched throat was irritated by it. He spat it out and stomped on it, gazed for a long time out over the desert, then left his drowsing animal and walked out where the brush was thickest. There he squatted with his back to the west, looking down toward the place where Curtin's crew was.

The wait was long. He began to fear he had guessed wrong; then the wiry figure materialized out of the brush at his side and hunkered.

"Why don't you just ride ahead, Guillermo?" Juan Soldado said softly.

Will shook his head in spite of his weariness. The Apache's scorn and dislike were plain. "No," he said in Spanish, "you know what the other white people would think. I'm working to keep your rancheria secret from them."

"Yes, but these men . . ." The Indian made a bitter, contemptuous gesture. It was eloquent and Will understood. He refused to discuss the topic further, though.

"I didn't think you'd be here. I thought you'd be far away with the people. I thought the decoy warrior might show up — not you."

"Huh!" Juan grunted and settled lower on the ground. He had a dragoon pistol stuffed into his

131

belt and a scuffed old carbine lying across his legs. "The people know where our hunting grounds are as well as I do. There are sub-chiefs. They will take them over there well enough. I am here with nine warriors."

"Nine?" Will said, surprised. There had been no tracks or signs.

Juan smiled ruefully. "One never knows what will happen in times like these, Guillermo. Besides, I thought we might give them a fight if we could lure them far enough away."

Will studied the dark, seamed profile in silence. Juan Soldado, however, didn't turn and look at Will. Finally the Indian grunted and fished out a ragged slip of paper.

"Here, this came back from Tucson, from that runner I sent with your paper-that-talks."

Will spread the wrinkled letter on his knee and carefully smoothed it out. The heavy black scrawl leaped off the paper at him. It was an indignant note, each line of the writing showing the writer's anger. Juan Soldado gazed in silence at Will's face, then down at the paper. There was bafflement and vast wonder in his expression.

"What does it say?"

"It says about what I guessed, Juan. The man who wrote this note is Judge Curtin, of Tucson. The man in Melton who says he's Judge Curtin isn't."

"A white man's lie," Juan Soldado said blandly. "What else does it say?"

"That this real Judge Curtin is getting up a

posse and coming over to Melton. It also says he sent a man to Melton two weeks ago to contact the people in the village to see about getting his nephews back."

Juan Soldado looked up in puzzlement at Will's face. "I don't understand this," he said.

Will folded and pocketed the letter and shook his head. "I don't either. Not altogether anyway. I guessed there was something wrong about this Judge Curtin in Melton, so I had you send that note to Tucson asking about him, explaining that there was a man who called himself Judge Curtin in Melton. I also told what he was doing over here."

"Ah! Then this real man over in Tucson is angry because another uses his name."

"Yes, but there's more to it than that."

"What?"

Will didn't answer Juan right away. He was staring in a brooding way down toward the darkness where Curtin's riders were. When he spoke it wasn't to answer Juan Soldado's question at all.

"Are the boys all right?"

"*Sí,* they are with the people. I left them in the care of my young wife. She's good to them."

"Fine. I want you to do two more things, Juan; then I believe our troubles will be over."

"Name them."

"First, I want you to take another letter to this man in Tucson. You'll have to send a rider out right away. Tonight, in fact. The real judge may be starting out from Tucson before your warrior can get there, even. He'll have to watch along the roads and trails. Whatever happens, have him deliver this second letter."

"It will be delivered. What else?"

"Follow these men I'm leading until we're all back in Melton. Then spread your warriors around the village and don't let any riders leave the place. Make a surround and keep it until this other band of riders gets here from Tucson."

"You don't want these gunmen to escape from Melton before the other riders arrive, then?"

"That's it exactly."

"I will do it. I'll send for more warriors right away and have them trail us to Melton. We'll make the surround and keep it. We'll let the men from Tucson ride into Melton but we won't let anyone ride out until you signal that it is all right for them to go." Juan Soldado smiled. The plan appealed strongly to his Indian instincts. "Good. Now how will you signal us, Guillermo?"

"With a signal fire in the daytime. Two puffs of smoke mean you are to let them all ride out of Melton. Three puffs mean you are to bring in your men closer to the village and let the townsmen see you."

"Why would I do this?" Juan Soldado asked in a surprised tone.

Will's thoughtfulness was easy to see. He was slow to answer. He knew the Apaches were his only tool. If the pseudo judge guessed how he had been outwitted — which he certainly would do when Will came back without the Thorndike boys — he might make good his oft-made threat to sack Melton.

"Juan, if these gunmen in Melton see how they are surrounded by Apaches, they may give up any ideas of fighting they have. They'd know they couldn't get away. They'd also know what you'd do to them if they tried to battle clear of your warriors."

"I see," Juan Soldado said; then he grinned again wider than ever. "You don't want them killed; you want to outthink them. That's always best, I suppose. This time I agree — but my men would like very much to fight them a little." Juan arose and held his carbine lightly, looking into the night. "I will have everything done as you want, Guillermo." He remained lost in thought for a moment; then he glanced down at the white man who was scribbling a note. "What about the little white boys? I could have them brought back too."

Will got up. "All right. I didn't think of that. It's best, I suppose. Keep them until I send up four smoke puffs, then." Will looked into the shorter man's face. "All right?"

"Bueno, Guillermo."

He gave Juan Soldado the note, then went back to the camp and aroused the sprawled gunmen with several barked orders for them to saddle up. His own mount required nothing more than a tug of the latigo and he was ready. Tom Elmore was one of the first to mount up and wheel in behind him. He had a solidly implacable look to his face that Will didn't miss.

They struck out again. This time there wasn't a sound at all except for the muffled tread of shod horses. The way lay southeasterly until Will saw the great, glowering bulwarks of the Galiuros dropping away on his left; then he knew the trail ahead as well as any Apache did.

He also knew that Elmore's riders would recognize the landmarks as soon as dawn came and that he rode with no advantage over them any longer. His peril increased with every forward step now. As long as he had stood as their only hope for salvation, he had nothing to worry about. Now, however, they could find their way back to Melton without him. His mind was going over the altered situation when the sun broke over the jagged offsets that were the pinnacles in the faintly seen east.

Tom Elmore rolled his head from side to side as the pink dawn widened its scope of light. Very slowly a satisfied look replaced his stormy expression and he nudged his tottering horse up beside Will with a cruel fierceness in his eyes.

"Graham, you've had your way up to now."

Will recognized the imminence of trouble. His wide blue eyes didn't waver. "Not quite. Curtin told me to leave you men here and go back for the Thorndike boys."

That made Elmore's savage stare dim a little. It was as though the gunman were torn between his own personal dislike of Will and his reluctance to cross Curtin. Will watched the inner conflict and waited. He suspected — in fact had planned it this way on the strength of his belief — that Tom Elmore wouldn't go against Curtin's orders.

The gunman swung his head and tilted it a little, gazing far ahead where the village was. He ran a pink, damp tongue around his badly cracked lips before he looked back at Will again.

"You can't do it."

"What can't I do?"

Elmore nodded toward Will's horse. "You can't ride back out there again on that horse. He's about bushed."

Will frowned over his answer. "I'm not going to do it on this horse," he said. "That's why I'm still with you. If I'd been going to split off I'd've done it before dawn."

"Before we knew where we were, eh?"

Will ignored the sarcasm. "Yes." He threw another long look at Tom Elmore's face and saw the doubt vanish and a crafty look replace it.

"All right. We'll all ride on in together."

Without another word Elmore pulled up and let Will ride away from him. Will didn't understand what the killer had in mind but he knew from Elmore's expression that the gunman had developed an alternative plan to his former one. Their fight was postponed but not forgotten. He kept his sore eyes shielded beneath his hat brim, fixed and motionless, watching for Melton to show up on the horizon, and tried to guess whether Tom Elmore constituted a real threat to him or not.

When the heat was rolling down over the desert, they were within sight of the village. Several of the riders croaked out pitiful little bleats of triumph. Will said nothing. He rode a few hundred feet ahead of them, right up to the outskirts of Melton; then two of the dehydrated skeletons kicked out their lurching horses and made a wobbly entrance into the hamlet to the accompaniment of heart-felt curses from their companions, who were irritated by this senseless abuse of horseflesh.

Will rode directly to the old Maxwell barn, dismounted, watered and rubbed down his mount. After he was stalled and fed he removed his own shirt and washed with a deep sense of luxury in the water trough, then struck uptown for Grady Stewart's trading post.

He had accomplished a little of what he had set out to do. The hardest part, he knew, would be to keep Curtin's renegades — and their chief — from taking any action at all for another day or so.

Grady was leaning vacant-eyed against an upright under the ramada when Will came up. The trading post was deserted. The trader turned his head and gazed a long silent moment at Will, then spat at a flitting lizard near his feet.

"You look like you been broiled, Will. I see you found 'em all right."

"Wasn't much trouble, Grady. Tracked the fools."

"Was it like you figured? The Indians were playin' with 'em?"

"Just about like I figured, Grady. Where's the judge?"

"Judge!" Grady said derisively. "I'm ashamed o' myself, Will, for not seeing through him like you did."

"Maybe you haven't had the experience with people that I've had. Anyway, it doesn't matter. Is he around?"

"Over at their camp as far as I know." Grady shoved off the post and rammed his fisted hands deep into his pockets. "That Mike Allen's been stinkin' drunk since the morning you left. There's a lot of tension in town all of a sudden, Will. It's bad."

Will watched the sweat drip off Grady Stewart's face. The same old Grady. Monotony was the worst thing in the world for him. Will turned and looked at the village. It was the same: dogs sprawled in their sleep, panting; Mexican adobes without a sign of life under the dazzling, brassy sunlight; no sound, no movement. It was always the same; no tomorrows. . . . He turned and let out a dry sigh.

"Where's Karen? Inside?"

"Yeah. Going over the books on those danged pledges."

Will left Grady to his moodiness and went inside the trading post. The smells of the place were pleasant to him after the arid, coppery odors of the burnt land. He had to wait for his eyes to become accustomed to the perpetual gloom of the place. While he stood in the shade, Karen looked up and saw him. He looked as if he had lost ten pounds. His normally thick-thewed, powerful body was thinned down. His face was almost the color of ancient leather. His lips were netted with tiny splits where dried blood showed, and his eyes looked swollen.

"Will."

He smiled with his face but not his mouth. The lips would crack open.

She had some lemonade and took him a tepid glass of it. He drank it and bit back the curse that arose over the sting of the stuff against his mouth. She stood gazing at him with a troubled, worried look. He had the same imperturbable, confident expression, but the rest of him looked exhausted and worn out.

"You need rest, Will," she said in a gentle, wondering voice. "I don't see how you keep it up."

He could see her easily now and his eyes suddenly felt rested at the vision. The room was shadowy-cool and very pleasant. He had a strange thought that filtered down into his awareness without his knowing what had prompted it or where it came from. If he had a choice as to where he would spend Eternity, it would be in this cool, drowsy atmosphere. He thought of Grady's mounting antipathy for the trading post and wagged his head in simple wonder at it.

"What're you shaking your head about?"

"Nothing," he said, looking down at her. "Nothing important anyway. What's new around here, Karen?"

"The same thing. The judge has kept strictly to himself since you left. Mike Allen's been to see me twice, and both times he's been so drunk I asked Grady to run him off. The others — I think Judge Curtin keeps them away from us. At any rate, they only come here for a drink; then they leave and go back to their camp. There's something in the air, Will. It frightens me a little."

Will felt for his tobacco sack. The lemonade was doing its work. He was perspiring like a horse. The water literally dripped off him. He lit up and regarded her through the smoke. He was going to speak but she beat him to it.

"Did you see the Indians?" He nodded without expression. "And the little boys?" Another nod. Exasperatedly, she flashed him a testy look. "You can be the most closed-mouthed person I've ever seen when you want to be."

"Comes from long habit," he said.

"And a hurt you won't forget," she said brutally, wanting to jar him a little, and succeeding.

His smile faded a little at a time until the slits of his eyes over the tendril of smoke were looking down into her face without friendliness in them, almost with antagonism. "Are you still digging, Karen?" he asked quietly.

"Yes, you could say I am," she said bluntly.

"That's what it takes to shake you out of yourself sometimes, Will."

"Why do you want to shake me out of myself, anyway?"

"Because you're in the habit of looking at people — through them — and thinking your thoughts without speaking. It's a bad thing out here. You ought to know that. When men grow silent and introspective, my father used to say, they'd better leave the desert or stop wearing guns."

"He should've known," Will said. Then he leaned back against the wall and pushed back his hat. She could see the sweat-plastered look of his hair, shades darker with moisture.

"He *did* know." She moved swiftly around him and dropped down on the wall bench. "Can't you forget her?"

Irritated, he cast a sharp look down at her. The way her head was tilted cut him under the heart somewhere and made a strange and unruly restlessness rise up to bother him. "I wasn't thinking of 'her,' Karen. I haven't thought of her for several weeks now."

"What is it, then? The Thorndike boys and Judge Curtin?"

"Yes."

Her gaze fell away from his face. The troubled look remained in her eyes. "And I've been worrying about Grady," she said softly.

He crushed out the cigarette and tossed it through the open doorway with a grunt. Grady was the least of his worries. He sank down on the bench beside her and pushed his legs out full length and let his eyelids droop. It was awfully pleasant there. The scent of her came vaguely to him. It was a smell of good soap and sage. His tired mind contrasted it with the wild mint scent of Apache women. The contrast made his mouth pull up in a sardonic little smile.

"Grady'll be all right," he said indifferently, slowly.

"No, he won't," she said right back with conviction and spirit. "He's drinking more than ever, Will."

It was incongruous. Here they all were, sitting atop a dynamite keg, with Apaches gathering reinforcements and surrounding Melton, with a madman calling himself Judge Curtin willing to turn his lawless band loose on them, with an angry man and more gunmen riding from Tucson spoiling for trouble — and Karen was worried over the amount of whiskey Grady Stewart drank!

He stirred a little and smiled crookedly. "All right, we'll start minding Grady's business when this other mess is over with." He let his eyes close completely and sighed. "I've got to go see the judge in a little while. Wake me up in a couple of hours, will you, Karen?"

She took his right hand and held it tightly between both of her palms. He was vividly conscious of her coolness and closeness. It was as though an electric shock had passed through

143

him. He opened his eyes and gazed at her sombrely.

"You'd better not do that," he said, withdrawing his hand. "Seems I said we'd go for a walk the evening of the day I rode out of here. How about moving that up to tonight?"

She didn't answer but got up and walked back over toward the thumb-smudged old ledgers behind the counter and dropped down at the table with a far-away look in her eyes. She sat there gazing out through the barred window behind her at the shimmering desert.

Will slept like a log until the boards began to dig into him; then he squirmed around, stretched out full length on the bench and dozed off again. After that he was conscious of nothing in this world until just before evening, when Karen washed his face with a cool rag. He opened his eyes and looked up at her. The shadows were deeper in the room. He knew the day was dying before she spoke.

"Here's some lamb stew, Will. I had the Mexicans haul in the big tub and fill it with water. You need a bath."

He sat up and dug at his eyes. They ached but didn't pain. "Do you have a lot of that stew?" he asked in a tired way. "I could eat a whole sheep if someone'd hold its head."

She watched him eat ravenously and thought that, even with the swollen look to his eyes and lips, the beard-stubble and desert dust, he was handsome. When he was finished she took away the bowl and herded him toward the curtained-off room where the big tub awaited.

He bathed and felt a hundred percent better. While he sat hunched up in the tub he contemplated the far wall and estimated the time required for the real Judge Curtin to get to Melton. That was how much time he'd have to stall any positive action by the renegades now investing the village.

Re-dressed, rested and fed, he was rejuvenated. When he was stooping to pick up his hat, Grady entered the room, appraised his freshly shaved cheeks and shiny-clean look, grunted and sank onto a little three-legged stool.

Will studied Grady's face closely and saw what Karen had probably seen also. The slightly more pronounced look of inner dissolution surprised him a little, making him feel uncomfortable, as though he were looking at Stewart's naked soul. Embarrassed, he looked away when Grady spoke.

"Curtin was looking for you, Will. I told him you were resting up."

"Thanks. He didn't say what he wanted, did he?"

Grady made a wry face. "Not to me, he didn't." Grady lifted his glance. It was a speculative look, full of unrest. "I think there's going to be trouble."

Will turned fully and watched Grady's expression. There was the same restlessness there, but also a little tincture of something that could have been apprehension.

"What makes you think that, Grady?"

"Well, my horse corral's behind the post, you know. From there I can see their camp real good. I saw some of those gunmen going over a big map with Curtin. One of 'em was that Tom Elmore feller." Grady's morose look held. "Why would they be studying a map, Will, unless it was of this country hereabouts or unless they were planning a raid against Apaches — or something like that?"

Will nodded. "Let 'em plan, Grady. They don't know where the Apaches are. All they'll do is ride themselves down again, and I've got a notion some of those gunmen don't like all this heat and sweat. Mostly they're saloon toughs. After what they went through yesterday and last night — I wouldn't be surprised if some of them pulled stakes."

"They can't do that," Grady said. "Whether they like it or not they've got to stick it out here. They aren't so dumb they don't know what'd happen if they was to try and ride away — four or five of 'em."

"That's right."

"Then they'll do what Curtin's paying them to do."

"Hunt Apaches?" Will said lightly. "Let 'em. They won't find an Indian that doesn't want to be found."

"You sure?"

"Absolutely sure, Grady."

146

The trader began to drum softly on the bench. His eyes grew remote, baffled. He wasn't looking at Will when he spoke again. "That might even be worse. I've got a feeling Curtin might just plunder Melton if things don't go his way."

"That possibility," Will said flatly, "exists. He as well as told me he'd do that."

"I was thinking like that, Will," Grady said, "and if it came to a choice I believe I'd rather have the Apaches do it."

Will looked briefly at the shadows. The evening was well advanced. He'd wasted this day well enough. If he could manage to do as much with the next two days there was an excellent chance that his plan might work after all. He strode past Grady and let his fingers trail lightly over the trader's slumped shoulder as he paused.

"How much liquor do you have on hand?"

Grady looked up at him defensively. "Why? You think I'm drinkin' too much?"

Will heard the antagonism and shook his head. "I wasn't thinking of that at all. I was wondering if you could manage to get most of Curtin's crew good and soused tonight; if you had enough liquor to do it."

"Oh," Grady said, looking back down at the floor with a little flush reddening his face, "I reckon I've got that much all right. You want to get 'em drunk for a purpose?"

"Yeah, to stall Curtin another day if I can."

Grady arose and rubbed his sweaty palms

against the seams of his trousers. "You got a plan, Will?"

"Yes, I think I have. I hope so, anyway."

"Sure, I'll get 'em lit up, then."

Will reached out and gave Grady's arm a squeeze, then went outside. The twilight was gone. Stars were winking overhead in the darkening sky. The smells of the desert were getting stronger, sweeping in upon Melton with a soft, fragile fragrance that was peculiar to the desert country, bringing with them the faintest scent of flowers that bloomed hidden beneath scalding boulders and in the secret, shady places where erosion was carving out vast crevices in the lined old hide of this ageless land.

Will breathed in deeply. An ironic thought came to him: that everything in the desert had boundless patience but man — the least durable, least predictable, least tractable inhabitant of the country.

He stepped out from under the ramada's overhang and waited until a stooped old Mexican trudged by leading an equally stooped and ancient burro loaded with faggots, before he swung through the hock-high dust toward the old barn where his horse was.

The animal was standing with lower lip hanging listlessly as it dozed. He threw up his head momentarily at Will's approach, caught the familiar scent and went back to dozing. Will led him down the murky old alleyway to the watering trough, waited until he was full and led him back, forked over another big bait of hay and left him to eat or sleep, as he chose. The country out behind the old barn was inky. He threaded his way among the debris and rubbish of a generation and walked steadily toward the ghostly outlines of the Curtin camp.

Twice dogs growled at his passing but were too lethargic to investigate him, and once a smoking Mexican, leaning against the adobe wall of his house with only the whites of his eyes and the glowing tip of his cigarette showing, spoke in his soft, musical tongue, bidding Will a good evening. Beyond the last hovel was the gunmen's camp. Will studied it briefly, then went toward Curtin's quarters.

Chapter 7

Judge Curtin looked steadily at Will without any expression at all when the younger man entered his tent. His grey eyes followed each movement of his visitor until Will was sitting in one of the chairs. Then the judge's arms bulged as he pushed his own chair around so that he was facing Will, and he spoke.

"Pretty long in coming over, Graham." There was an evenness to the words that was like the cutting edge of a knife.

Will's answer was as even. "You ought to ride out into that desert a few times, Judge. You'd appreciate what it takes out of a man then."

Curtin folded his hands in his lap and never once let his eyes stray away from Will's face. "Where are the kids I sent you after?"

"I had to come back for a fresh horse. Elmore'll tell you the shape mine was in. In fact, it was Elmore who said I'd never make it if I rode back after we got within sight of Melton."

"So — more delay."

"It can't be helped," Will said, feeling his stomach muscles tightening against the definite menace in the older man's glance. "I'll ride out at dawn. That's the best I can do."

"It's taking too much time."

There was a finality to the way Curtin said it that made Will's defenses come up swiftly. "There's no other way, I'm afraid."

"No? I think there is." Curtin leaned forward and rested his arms on the table. "I think Tom's got a pretty good idea of this country. He and I've talked it out pretty well. He thinks he knows about where he can find Apaches." Curtin paused. "He's going out before dawn and catch us a few of the lousy devils — alive."

"You're back to that," Will said sardonically. "It isn't good sense, Judge. You not only won't catch any Indians; you'll get some men killed."

"Not when fifteen go out, I won't," Curtin said, "and I'll give you odds Tom'll come back with some buck Indians, too."

There was no point in talking about it. Will could see with half an eye that Curtin had his mind made up. He felt like swearing at the man; instead, he studied the lean, tight-skinned face with its dry-looking, icy grey eyes and wondered what the man was up to, and who he was.

"Tom's pretty hostile, Graham. You know that, don't you?"

"It's no secret. He makes a point of letting me know it."

"He's pushing hard for a little party he wants me to sanction — where you're concerned."

"Why don't you let him have his party, Judge?" Will was baiting Curtin. He knew he'd struck pay dirt when the grey-eyed renegade flushed darkly. Curtin, Will felt quite certain, wasn't sure yet that he couldn't use Will somehow. So long as he felt that way he'd be reluctant to see Will injured.

"Graham, maybe it's like Tom says. You're too cussed smart for your own good."

"No, hardly that, Judge. I'm not looking for trouble. You and Elmore are. If he's dead set on stirring up something, let him."

"You're pretty fast, is that it?"

"Average," Will said, "just average. If you really want to find out, turn Elmore loose."

It was partly bluff but it worked. Curtin relaxed and sat back in his chair again. For a moment or two he said nothing and studied Will's face. "I'm not sure you're not playing some game of your own, Graham."

"Like what?" Will asked. Then he made a derisive sound. "How would I do it, outnumbered twenty to one?"

"That's what I told Tom," Judge Curtin said. "He swears he saw moccasin tracks where you sat under some brush, out on the desert a night ago."

Will was shaken by that. He hadn't seen Tom Elmore go anywhere near where he and Juan Soldado had hunkered, talking. It annoyed him a little to think he'd underestimated the gunman.

"Maybe Elmore's seeing Indians in the shadows now."

"Maybe," Curtin said, but without conviction. "Maybe you're smarter than I think you are, too. Well, I'm not going to mess around with you any more, Graham. You've had your chances and you haven't produced. Now I'll work things my way."

Will shrugged and said nothing. He had a feeling of uneasiness. He wanted in the worst way to know what lay behind Curtin's plans. He had proved himself a wily adversary. Will knew whatever he did would have been carefully planned beforehand.

"Maybe Tom's imagining Indians and maybe he isn't. Maybe, too, you could take him out and show him some."

"I doubt that very much."

"I don't. You know 'em. We all know that. I've got a hunch you're hand in glove with 'em. I don't think Tom imagined that Apache moccasin track either, Graham. In fact, I've got it all planned for you to lead the boys out before dawn tomorrow and scout up some Apaches for 'em. That — or else."

Will was wooden-faced. The same threat again. He knew what the "or else" meant. Now he considered it objectively for the third time. There still was no way to circumvent the judge with any degree of caution. Not as far as Grady and Karen and the innocent Mexicans of Melton were concerned.

Curtin frowned. "Tom even thinks you could get those Thorndike boys if you wanted to. I don't know about that. Wish I did; it'd make things easier for me. Graham, Tom wants to wring it out of you."

"How could I ride a horse tomorrow if you did that?" Will asked, his anger rising.

"That's it exactly: you couldn't. Will, we're buffaloed there, but I'm going to tell you something else. When you ride out of Melton before dawn tomorrow, your chances of ever coming back again are doggoned slim. Tom's after your heart. I'm the only thing that stands between you and him. If you show him Indians he'll let you come back not too badly hurt. If you get those boys, he's agreed to leave you strictly alone. If you don't do either . . ." Curtin shrugged.

"It's up to you, Graham."

"I see." Will looked at the furnishings of the tent with a detached air. There were guns and telescope carpet bags. Driving harness was piled carelessly in a jumble of traces and lines in one corner.

"You don't seem worried, Graham."

Will got up. "Should I be?" he asked. "Seems to me you and Elmore've already worked things out to suit yourselves, Curtin. Worrying isn't going to help any, is it?"

Curtin's anger rose in the face of Will's calmness. His mouth flattened against his teeth and hardly moved when he spoke. "I don't like being baited, Graham. You might push a man a little too far."

"I won't have to do that, Curtin. You're doing it yourself. You'll see what I mean when the time comes."

Curtin stood up abruptly. His face was dark with a rush of angry blood. "I can break you pretty easily, Graham," he said. "I can do better'n that. I can wreck this village until there isn't enough left of it to make kindling out of. I'm going to do it, too — you have my word on that — if you come back tomorrow without Apache captives."

Will looked at the scarcely controlled fury in Curtin's face and felt inexpressibly calm himself. "Why, Judge?" he asked. "Why are you doing this?"

"That's none of your business."

Will stood there looking at the man's face and pondering its fury a moment longer. "Why don't we stop maneuvering, Judge? Why do you want those boys?"

"I've told you that."

"But it wasn't the truth," Will said coldly, measuring the man's wrath and playing with it. "You don't care about the kids. I knew that the day you sent men out to track me after I told you what'd happen to the boys if you did."

"The Thorndike boys," Curtin said with an effort to keep a rein on his temper, "are important to me."

"All right, I know that. So are the Apaches. But why?"

Curtin's eyes were still and unmoving. Very slowly his mouth closed and the bulge of jaw muscles corded the lower portion of his face.

"I'll hazard a guess for you, Judge. You're

after some information the Thorndike boys have about a copper mine; at least about a possible location of a copper mine. You figure if you can get the Thorndike boys they'll have that information. Failing their apprehension, you're thinking that the Apaches will have found out from the boys where this vein is. Is that right?"

Curtin lowered himself to the chair again. His steady unblinking regard of Will was like the lidless stare of a rattlesnake. "Graham," he said gently, enunciating very clearly, "you've stuck your beak in where it's got no business. You've asked for a killing for a long time. I've held Tom off but I don't think I'll hold him off any longer."

"Won't you?" Will said, still standing, his thumbs hooked in his shell-belt. "I'm gambling that you will, Curtin."

"Then you've lost a bet."

"In that case," Will said coldly, "you'll not only never get those boys back; in addition, you'll never see an Apache nor the copper vein either."

He watched Curtin's face closely, but the renegade had closed off all expression and sealed it over with a blank stoniness. Will was wondering inwardly if he hadn't gone too far. Still, what he'd said was perfectly true. If Curtin had him killed . . . His personal knowledge of the Apaches was his ace-in-the-hole. He meant to save it only to save Melton.

"So Tom was right. You were seeing Apaches right along."

"Tom's guess is no better than yours, Curtin. I'll tell you this much though. Right from your first day here you've pushed this affair in the face of those who know better how to work it. I'm not going to try and talk you out of your own way of doing it. I'm just going to tell you this. I'll ride out with your boys in the morning — those who'll be able to ride — and if you'll make a trade with me, I'll show 'em Apaches. But the first hostile move from you or Elmore will be the last, as far as I'm concerned."

"You have nothing to trade, Graham."

"Yes, I have. I'll trade you the information you want for the truth of this affair."

Curtin's eyes flickered. "Do you know where that vein is?"

"No, but I can find out pretty easily."

"That's your trade? You'll find out and tell me, in exchange for what's behind my plans?"

"Yes."

"You can go to blazes, Graham. Tom Elmore'll send you there after you lead him to the Apaches. That's your answer."

Will wasn't altogether surprised at Curtin's violent refusal. "In that case, Judge, call him in here and let him fire away, because I won't lead them to the Apaches tomorrow."

Curtin looked dourly at Will. "That's a useless bluff, Graham."

"If you think I'm bluffing, call Elmore in."

Curtin's expression became slightly less assured. His gaze hung curiously on Will's face.

There was a long moment of silence while the men faced one another over the impasse. Will was gambling, and yet in a sense he was perfectly sincere. It wasn't his nature to throw down challenges without meaning them.

"Your play, Judge."

"You're a fool, Graham. I can find Apaches without you."

"I reckon you can. You can also pull their tongues out by the roots and they'll tell you nothing. And there's something else you're overlooking. I'm the only one who can get those boys back. Either way you'll lose."

"That's why you think your offer of a trade's so good, is it?"

"Right."

Curtin's glance swung away from Will's face for the first time since the younger man had entered the tent. It went to the door flap and stayed there for a moment.

"What'll you guarantee for this trade, Graham?"

"To find out where that copper vein is and ride back here with the information."

He almost smiled at the quick look of craftiness that whipped over Curtin's features, then disappeared as suddenly as it had come.

"Well," the judge said, "I'm going to trade with you, but not for the reasons you think. In the first place I've got a guarantee you'll be back — the girl and Stewart. If you're not back within twenty-four hours I'll have their gullets slit from ear to ear." He paused to let that soak in, then went on again, looking almost as though he were enjoying this.

"And you're pretty danged clever, Graham. I told you once before you and me'd make a good team. All right, I'll take you for a pardner on your own terms so's we'll be working together in this. Later, there'll be other things."

Will kept his face impassive although Curtin's abrupt reversal seemed ironic to him. He had seen that flash of wiliness when he'd told Curtin he'd let him know the location of the copper vein. When Curtin knew where the vein was he'd have Will dry-gulched on the spot. It was that simple and Will knew it.

"Now then, how soon can you get the location for us?"

"Maybe tomorrow," Will said; "maybe the day after tomorrow."

"It's got to be sooner."

"It can't be, Curtin. I've got to ride a good hundred miles there and back just to find the Apaches. This is summer. If you don't know what that means on the desert, you ought to."

"I don't like the delay."

"Neither do I," Will said not very truthfully, "but there's no other way. I'll make it as fast as I can." He ran a hand over his forehead to swipe away some drops of perspiration. "Now tell me what all this hurry is about, will you?"

"All right," Curtin said, leaning on the table and looking up at Will again, his little eyes like steel agates. "In the first place I'm not Judge Curtin of Tucson. I used that name over here for reasons of prestige. My real name's Matthews. That's enough for now."

"How'd you stumble onto this mine deal?"

"That wasn't hard. I own two saloons in Tucson. Judge Curtin used to stop in for a night-cap once in a while. He and I got to talking about gold one time. After that we visited over the bar and I dug out of him what him and his brother-in-law were doing. Copper, nothing! They called it copper for safety's sake. They were after gold. When I heard what'd happened to Thorndike, and who had the boys, I figured the kids might remember where they'd been out here, so I got together a crew and rode over. Now you'll know what my hurry is. I don't know whether old Curtin's doing anything or not, but I don't want to wait until he does before I stake a claim on that gold his brother-in-law was after."

"How did you know there was any gold?"

Matthews snorted disdainfully. "Heck, Graham, the old judge and that sharp-shootin' brother-in-law of his weren't greenhorns. They've got other mines. Thorndike wouldn't have risked a run into Apacheria, almost using the old Apache Trail itself, unless he had darned good information that there was gold where he was heading."

Will stood there thinking it over. The dead brother-in-law had been more than a fool, in his opinion, to subject his wife and sons to the

Indian menace at any time, but when the Apaches were "out," he was guilty of criminal negligence in doing it. But he had done it and that was that.

"Gold," he said. "I thought it was copper."

Matthews looked up swiftly. "What made you think that?"

"The boys. I talked to them."

"You *what?*"

"Talked to them in an Apache rancheria."

"The devil you did." Matthews' astonishment wasn't feigned. "What did they say? Do they remember where they went?"

"Yes, they said they remembered all right, only I wasn't interested enough to ask them."

"Likely," Matthews said brusquely.

"I thought it was copper, not gold. Copper means nothing to me."

Matthews got up again; only this time he walked back and forth between the tent wall and his table with short, springy steps. "Blast that Elmore," he said finally. "He almost had me talked into eliminating you. Listen, Graham, you lead my boys out after Apaches tomorrow. I want it done this way. If that fails, we'll send you among 'em again." The grey eyes were swift-moving now, and an avaricious fire burned steadily in their depths. Will saw the change and was surprised by it. He hadn't associated greed with Matthews before. A lot of other things, but not greed. He turned toward the flap and held it open with one hand, turned his head and looked back at the renegade, the other hand resting lightly on his holstered gun. He debated arguing against Matthews' Apache hunt. A long look at the older man's face convinced him of the futility of such a course right then. He sighed.

"Have Elmore awaken me at the old barn where I keep my horse about dawn. Agreed?"

"Agreed," Matthews said. Will walked back out into the night.

He went back across the village toward the trading post. Long before he got there he heard the bedlam and stopped, making a stocky silhouette in the purple shadows, listening. There was a wolfish look to his face now. Grady was doing his duty, judging from the sounds of the men inside the post.

He bypassed the post and swung wide in order to avoid the loop-legged traffic that was ebbing and flowing in the night. Walking in a big circle around through the Mexican hovels, he came to Karen's little adobe and knocked at the door.

When she was satisfied who it was and came outside, his breath caught in his throat. She was wearing a tight blouse and a full, flowing skirt that rustled when she moved. Her hair shone dully in the gloom and her eyes were liquid-clear so that the moonlight caught in them and was imprisoned there. She was looking up into his face.

Without a word he took her arm, piloted her down a little back alley such as was common to Mexican villages, and led her among the discarded wagon wheels, moldering pieces of harness and broken pots until they were beyond the raucous reach of the noise from the trading post. There, they went out into the dusty, crooked thoroughfare and, as though by mutual accord, headed toward the crumbling, forlorn little church.

The south end of Melton was steeped in a hush of eternal drowsiness. He used his hat to brush the dust off the adobe steps and watched her sit down. Dropping down beside her, he looked over into her face.

"Is this where you wanted to come?"

She answered as though to speak loudly would be a form of blasphemy. "Yes, I love it down here."

"It's quiet all right," he said, looking out into the night where the squatty, dark outlines of the distant *jacals* were.

"It's more than that, Will. This is the way Melton used to be when I was a little girl; quiet and sleepy and peaceful."

"No Apaches?" he asked.

"Apaches? Yes, there were always Apaches. At least the knowledge that they were out in the night somewhere. But that wasn't any worse to a little girl than the vague knowledge that death was out there, too. When you're very young those are distant things, I think." She looked over at him, studied his face in the gloom. "Did you see Curtin?"

"Now you're fishing again, aren't you?"

"I won't if it's a secret."

He chuckled at the sound of irritation in her voice. "It's no secret. I saw him all right. In fact, it's the only time I've ever seen him that I enjoyed it." He let his head go back so he could look into the starry night. "He and I made a trade — only he doesn't know I have no intention of keeping any part of my end of it."

"The Thorndike boys?"

"Indirectly, they enter into it, but they aren't the crux of it." In order to sidestep more discussion, he cocked his head to listen to the distant, night-borne sounds of revelry up at the trading post. "Do you reckon," he asked dryly, "that Grady's getting the riders drunk?"

She sniffed and looked away from him, her face somber. "I know he is. Liquor is a bad thing, Will. Grady'd be a successful business man if it weren't for whiskey."

"Not this time, Karen. He's doing that because I asked him to. I want him to get those hombres so drunk they'll be sick and staggering come dawn."

"Why?" She looked downright startled.

"I'm supposed to lead them out after Apaches tomorrow and I don't want to. If they're too sick and hung over to go, Curtin'll have to postpone it for another day. That's what I've got in mind."

"A delay. . . . But why?"

He got up suddenly and turned toward her, his arms out. "Let's walk a little."

She got up quickly and linked her arm through

his. They strolled south through the still, hot night to the end of the village and stood there in silence facing the threatening darkness that led into Mexico. Karen looked up at him.

"You're restless, aren't you?"

"Yes'm," he said, then rolled a cigarette, lighted it and let the smoke trail into the still air. "Restless."

"Do you want to talk about it?"

He looked around and down, guessing her thoughts. "It's not what you think it is — this restlessness."

"Not her?"

"No."

"But you do think of her?"

"Not lately," he said, looking at the glowing tip of the cigarette, "not since Curtin came to town."

"I'm glad," she said fiercely. Then in embarrassment she disengaged her arm from his and turned to look up the crooked roadway to the glowing distance where orange-yellow splashes of light spilled over into the dust from Grady Stewart's trading post. There were silhouettes limned up there, every now and then, but the sounds were almost lost to her. "Let's go back to the church."

They did. As he lowered himself beside her again, she laced her fingers around her knees and looked very gravely at the high, icy-looking stars and the capsized shape of the thin moon.

Will was sprawled on the broad step, his legs

pushed out before him. He was, she thought, as relaxed as a man could be. The stringy wisp of cigarette smoke drifted lazily up past his pushed-back hat.

"Karen," he said suddenly, "this is mighty pleasant."

She was going to say something other than what she did say. But a moving shadow across the road, among the huddled shapes of the adobes, gave rise to a tense comment. "There's a man over there. He's watching us."

Will raised his head almost indifferently. "I thought there might be," he said, and his teeth shone dully in the weak light. He was grinning.

"What does he want, Will?"

"Nothing important, Karen. Just wants to be sure I don't ride out of Melton tonight. Look — how far away do you reckon those stars are?"

She looked up instinctively. "Too far, Will."

"Couldn't we reach them if we tried very hard, Karen?"

When she didn't answer, the spell was broken and he lowered his gaze, saw the shadow across from them melt deeper into the night, and let his breath out as though it had been stored against this moment for a long time. She heard the sweep of it being expelled from his chest.

"Do you want to go back now?"

"I suppose we should," she said without much conviction. "It's a beautiful night, though."

He didn't move until the cigarette was finished and extinguished against the old adobe steps;

then he stood up and helped her to her feet and stood gazing down into the pale shadow that was her face, tilted a little, watching him.

"I never thought I'd ever want to do again what I want to do right now."

She knew. The honest clumsiness of the sentence was no barrier to understanding because she knew. It was almost as though she had been awaiting this moment all evening. He kissed her. His mouth moved over hers to avoid the broken, rough places in his lips and savor the cool velvet of her response.

She pushed a little, and he stepped back. Without a word she turned, took his arm and walked with him in complete silence until the bedlam at Grady's trading post broke in upon their flow of thoughts. Then she led him by a short-cut to her little adobe and stopped there, dropping his arm, waiting.

He felt as though he had always been doing this, had always been kissing Karen Maxwell. There was neither embarrassment nor discomfort nor uneasiness. He kissed her good-night and waited for the words she didn't find right away; then, when she spoke them in her gentle, wondering voice, he found they were old words, too.

"Are you going into the desert again, Will?"

"Afraid I'll have to, Karen."

"When you get back, come and see me. And remember I'm here, too. Don't be heroic out there, if you have to go."

He started to bend, but she put a finger against his mouth and pushed him away. He stopped. She ran her hand lightly over his face and went swiftly through the thick door, and he heard the *tranca* bar drop into place with a strong, solid sound.

Will went as far back uptown as the old barn. There he watered his horse, fed him again, although the animal hadn't yet finished his last bait of hay, then leaned on the old stall door, thinking.

There was a certain annoyance caused by the knowledge that Matthews had put one of his gunmen to watch him. He debated whether to catch the man or not. He decided against it, pushed around among the loose straws of the hay pile, punched a sleeping hole into the softest part and lay back, wide awake, staring out into the night. He knew the gunman would be along in a little while to see what he was up to, but that didn't bother him beyond a mild feeling of irritation. There were a lot of things to think about, and foremost among them was what Matthews' reaction to the condition of his men would be when they were supposed to roll out and saddle up before dawn.

Finally he heard the faint, hushed sound of footsteps, but didn't bother to turn until the man was close enough. Then he raised himself up and looked steadily at the crouched silhouette.

"Go on back and tell Curtin I'm in bed and that I'll be here come dawn."

The man slunk away without a word.

He turned on his side and lost consciousness.

It was as though he hadn't been asleep at all when someone shook his shoulder roughly. "Come on, Graham — time to get moving."

He brushed the hay away and looked up at Tom Elmore. The gunman's face was partly hidden in shadow, as though he were deliberately avoiding Will's gaze.

"Dawn'll be here in another hour or so."

Will pushed his way out of the hay, tugged his boots over swollen feet and grunted upright. "Have you rounded up the others yet?"

Elmore's face came around. It was inscrutably blank. "We'll do that together. Come on."

Will went out back to the water trough and washed methodically. He was aware of Elmore's mounting impatience and ignored it until he was ready to go; then they stalked through the dark barn toward the front roadway with only one more stop. Will forked more hay to his horse.

Outside, there was a slight chill in the predawn air. The smells of the desert were stronger, redolent with creosote bush and oily sage. Elmore kept a steady course toward the gunmen's camp and stopped when they came to the first bedroll. Will stopped one step behind the gunman. An aroma of green whiskey jumped out of the close night air and smote his nostrils sharply. He made a wry face and listened to Elmore's efforts to curse the others out of their bedrolls. They went together among all the sleeping men and repeated the process. The degrees of whiskey odor varied from strong to very strong. Grady Stewart had done his job well.

On the edges of the camp shadowy shapes that were moving men formed a phantom-like background. Tom Elmore threw a harsh grin at Will. "I warned 'em last night about that drinkin'. They'll ride whether they're drunk or sober. If I got to tie each one in his saddle, they'll ride."

Will got the impression there was a triumphant innuendo in the gunman's words. He wondered about it but said nothing until men began to form with their saddled horses; then he turned away from Tom Elmore with a casually flung sentence. "I'll go saddle up."

Back in the barn, he got his mount ready and frowned over the effort. Elmore and Matthews weren't going to be stymied by drunken riders. He swung up and wheeled out of the barn's low doorway, straightened in the saddle and gazed over to where a dark, writhing splotch resolved itself into men and horses. He looked out where the desert was, wondering if Juan Soldado would have driven his men ruthlessly and if by now the town would be surrounded. It made his lip curl upward a little. This wasn't exactly what he'd planned or wanted to happen, but it certainly would set the Matthews gunmen — and Matthews himself — back on his heels.

His own position wasn't enviable though. Gunmen behind — Apaches in front. Either side could and would kill him in the gloom of pre-dawn unless he was extremely careful. He thought of Karen's words and let his gaze wander down the still roadway as far as Grady's trading post.

"Ready?"

He turned and saw Tom Elmore coming toward him on a stocky bay horse. He lifted his reins, looking beyond Matthews' straw-boss. The gunmen were there; a long, lifeless line of them drifting over behind Tom Elmore. They looked badly used up and decidedly dejected. He looked back at Elmore and saw the man's hard triumphant leer.

"When they got a job to do, Graham, they'll do it. Maybe you figured otherwise."

Will turned his horse and struck out down the silent, shadowy roadway with the faint sound of many horses behind him. He went past Grady's ramada and thought he saw a man's shadow there. He wondered and strained to see, then swung on past.

Elmore kneed up beside him. His attitude was very clearly one of distinct and violent dislike, sheathed under a very thin veneer of restraint. It didn't fool Will a bit, nor did the gunman intend it to.

"Hope you can produce, Graham."

Will made a dry sound in his throat. "That's likely to be the last hope you'll ever have, Elmore."

The gunman's temper flared. "You won't

walk back, mister," he said. "If there's any monkey business you'll be the first to come apart. I promise you that."

Will looked into his savage gaze calmly enough. "I thought you wanted to fight Apaches. Seems to me Curtin said you were downright eager to shoot a few."

"I am. We all are. But you're a treacherous dog an' I told Curtin that. He gave me orders to blow your head off at the first sign of a double-cross. I'm looking forward to that, Graham. You know it now if you didn't figure it before."

"It won't even have to be a double-cross, Elmore. I know that, too."

"Do you?" the gunman asked. "Then I ain't giving you enough credit." Elmore's strong, even teeth showed briefly. "I reckon you know why I postponed our little fight yesterday, then. I got a better excuse now."

Will didn't answer. He rode out of Melton with his head hanging a little and with a tough, sharp set to his mouth. He had known he wasn't in a very good position, nor had he underestimated or forgotten Tom Elmore, but the full peril of his predicament hadn't come over him until this moment.

He looked up, after they were down the desert a mile or so, and saw the pale, diluted light of approaching dawn. If Juan Soldado and his warriors were out here — then it wouldn't be long now.

Chapter 8

Will led the riders farther out, and as the sun rose, so did his tension. Elmore was behind him, the killers behind Elmore and the Apaches somewhere up ahead. Heretofore he hadn't been in any serious danger, for his value to Matthews was sufficient to protect him. Tom Elmore, though, had none of Matthews' craftiness or foresight. To the gunman's direct approach there was only one answer. Either Will produced or he didn't. If he didn't, he died with a bullet in the back or in the face.

He kept his head up now. There was an ominous silence, a hush that was like the stillness of death. He didn't know whether the gunmen behind him felt it or not, but he did. No desert thrushes flittered from cactus to sage and back again. There was no movement and no sound in the cool half-light, the feeding time for desert denizens. It meant that men were about. Any frontiersman would have sensed it right away. Apaches!

Juan Soldado was out there somewhere all right. Will knew there were black eyes watching them from dark faces. His gaze strove to see in many directions at once.

"What you lookin' for, Graham?"

He heard and ignored Elmore's question. The fact that the killer was riding behind him was enough. Out of curiosity he swung in the saddle and bypassed Tom, with a long look of appraisal at the men behind him. Some were looking less ill than others, but with few exceptions none of them looked well nor fresh. He got a jolt when he saw Mike Allen riding in the drag of the straggling column.

Elmore swung too. He had a sardonic look when he faced forward again. "You didn't expect to see Mike along, did you?"

Will flickered a steady glance at Elmore. "No, why'd you bring him?"

Elmore nudged his horse around Will and up beside him as he answered, "The judge says Mike needs to be weaned away from the whiskey bottle."

"The judge," Will said flatly, "isn't a judge and you know it."

Elmore's cruel smile faded. "Who told you that?"

It was Will's turn to show sardonic, brittle amusement. "He did. Told me last night. His name's Matthews. Anything else you want to know?"

Elmore licked his lips quickly as though baffled by something. He didn't answer.

"He told me a lot of things, among them why he's here and what he wants. We made a pardnership."

"He didn't tell me that."

"I reckon there's a lot he hasn't told you, Elmore," Will said dryly. "Not that it matters." He was looking straight ahead when he said it, and the thing that prompted his last four words was a wisp of coppery movement, off to his right and about six hundred feet ahead.

As though intuitively sensing the meaning behind Will's words, Elmore straightened in his saddle and swung his head in a searching half-circle of the terrain. He saw nothing.

Someone behind them let out a deep shout. Will turned swiftly. He saw the reason for the shout before he saw the man who had made it. Little puffs of dark-oily smoke rose from a signal fire not half a mile west of Melton. He heard Tom Elmore's lungs empty of air in a loud whoosh.

"What the devil! There's Injuns out there."

Will heeded the words and looked back at the gunman. "Well, you want to ride over there?"

Elmore held up his hand. The strung-out column stopped, then began to close up. Bleary eyes and slack mouths grew steadier. Hands with damp palms and nervous fingers fondled carbines and six-guns. For the first time the gunmen saw evidence of the enemy they had made light of. It was a startling experience. Apaches within a half-mile of their camp back in Melton!

"Well?" Will said softly, watching Elmore.

The gunman slumped a little and looked over at him. His face, under its reddening sheen of perspiration, was tight-looking. "Did you know they were there?"

"Don't be ridiculous. No one ever knows where an Apache will show up."

"I don't like this — hanged if I do."

Will looked back toward the village. It was tiny in the distance. If he knew Juan Soldado, the Apaches would be in behind them now, cutting them off from Melton. They would be surrounded. Elmore's voice jarred into his thoughts.

"We got to get back."

"Why? You want to fight Indians. Let's ride over where they're signalling and see if there aren't a few around."

Elmore swore viciously at Will. His face was pale and his eyes shone dangerously. "You fool, they'll be behind us. We might even be surrounded by now." He paused and licked his lips again. "Graham, if you led us into this . . ." Another pause. "All right, mister, you ride back down the line and take the lead. Stay out in front all the way back. If anyone gets salivated it'll be you. Go on."

Will shook his head slowly back and forth. He felt none of the panic that the gunmen showed. "If you'll ride with me I'll do it. If you won't I'll stay right here."

With a rippling curse Elmore flashed his gun up over the swells of his saddle. The cocking mechanism made a sharp, loud sound. "Do like I said, Graham."

Will shook his head again. Their eyes were

locked. "Go ahead and shoot. The first shot'll be your last. It'll start the fighting. They're in behind us by now, all right. Go ahead — pull the trigger."

A man growled deep in his chest a short distance from Tom Elmore. He was watery-eyed and blue-lipped. Anger burned in his eyes as he looked at Elmore. "Put up that gun, Tom. You kill him and there'll be the devil to pay. Put 'er up!"

Elmore didn't. He held the gun and faced something he wasn't equipped to cope with — an impasse. Will held his glance as steady as a stone, waiting.

Several of the Matthews riders rode closer to the main group, and all of them sat facing back, silent. There wasn't a sound anywhere. Will could hear the sharp, ragged breathing of Elmore. He turned his head finally, sensing that the immediate peril was past, and watched the little smoke puffs. There were two, then an interval, then three more. He didn't know what they meant but suspected they were signals acquainting other Apaches with the approach of white gunmen.

When the second signal fire blossomed out with more little dark blobs of smoke, east of them. Will leaned on his saddlehorn with both hands and spoke to Elmore without looking at him.

"Take a squint behind you."

Elmore did, his gun still gripped in his fist, but

sagging. Two short puffs, a pause, then three fast ones.

"What's that mean?"

"I don't know, but I'd guess it means they're passing the word that we're out here."

"Cut off!"

Will shrugged. "It's a long way back. If they're between us and Melton we'll ride into an ambush by going back."

"Well, what else can we do?" Elmore holstered his gun and glared. "We can't keep on going. There's no water."

"No," Will said softly with a level glance at the sweating killer. "Can't go ahead. Can't go back. I reckon we fight, then."

Elmore's bafflement was complete. His eyes were bulging with indecision and apprehension. He swore often and blisteringly until Will had enough of it.

"That won't help. You wanted to fight Apaches. Came out to do it. Then let's go fight 'em."

"Not like this. This'd be murder. You can't see 'em to shoot at. There's nothin', Graham. No targets — no nothin'."

"I tried to explain that to both you and Matthews. You knew better." Will gestured slowly with his arm. "There are your Indians — out there in the brush somewhere." He let the arm drop.

The gunmen seemed to have lost their inertia almost as though by magic. Those who had been least alert among them were now steady-eyed and tight-mouthed.

Elmore lifted his reins. He was holding them in a fisted left hand. The knuckles showed white. "This is an ambush," he said. "Someone put 'em up to it, Graham."

"Don't be silly," Will shot back with scorn. "Apaches always fight like this. If you hadn't spent so much time in Matthews' saloons you'd know it. The evidence has been around you ever since you came to Arizona."

Will felt the heat boring into him. "Come on. We can't sit out here all day. Are we going ahead or going back?"

"Back. Where else could we go?"

"Nowhere," Will said calmly. "Then ride beside me and we'll see if we can get through 'em."

Tom Elmore's fury was acid within him. Every time he crossed Will Graham, he either had to back down or was turned aside. His loathing of Will was becoming more than hatred; it was becoming a mania with him, and yet he was motivated by the desire to save himself. Without a word he rode down the line of rigid, silent men at Will's side.

When they came to the tail end of the column, Will reined up and looked at Mike Allen. The fat man's face was wreathed in an unhealthy-looking pallor and was dewed with sweat. His eyes were puffy and running.

"Allen, stay behind me."

"What?"

"You heard me. Stay directly behind me." Will ignored Elmore's thundercloud expression and searched among the other faces for a man who looked less murderous than the others. He found him in the older rider who had trailed them from up front. "You — with the grey hair — stay behind Elmore. Don't let anyone else get in behind him and don't let him break away, either."

"What d'you mean by that, Graham?" Elmore's anger was thick in his throat. It affected his speech a little.

Will ignored him after the two men had placed themselves between the rest of the killers and him and Tom Elmore. A careful study of the country up ahead showed nothing. He hadn't expected it to. When you saw an Apache warrior he either wanted you to see him or you came upon him unexpectedly. They were the most deadly, the most thoroughly lethal, when you didn't see a single one.

"What you waiting for? Let's make a run for it."

Will shook his head and continued to sit there in plain view, out in front of the white men. "No, just be quiet for a while, Elmore."

"We're targets like this!"

"Maybe," Will said shortly, feeling the sweat running in rivulets under his shirt. "I'm doing this my way. If you don't like it, you can take over."

But Elmore wouldn't do that either. He sat

180

and sweated and a muscle in his neck jumped occasionally. Beyond that, though, he had gotten himself under control.

Will sat motionless for a half an hour. The sun bore down on all of them in the eerie silence, and finally he felt satisfied. If Juan Soldado was there — and Will knew he was — he would have seen Will by now. That meant he would restrain his warriors from firing on the mounted column of heavily armed gunmen until Will sanctioned such a course. When Tom Elmore's monotonous swearing had reached the point where he was repeating himself, Will threw him a withering look. The gunman lapsed into angry silence, then burst out into speech.

"What's the sense o' sitting here like sage-hens waiting to be potted, Graham?"

"No one's been potted yet, Elmore. Just shut up and do like I tell you."

A flash-flood of dark blood raced under Elmore's cheeks, but he kept silent.

Will lifted his reins and began a slow retreat. Not a one of the tight-lipped, suffering gunmen behind him tried to hurry the pace. They rode in uncommunicative silence, their eyes slitted against the merciless smash of sunlight, their hands closed tightly around pistol grips and carbine chambers. It was a strain, and every face showed it. When they had progressed beyond the place which Will had decided would be the most dangerous ground, and no bullets tore into them, he turned toward Elmore.

"Indian hunters! I told Matthews you boys'd get whipped the first time you crossed the Apaches — but darned if I thought it'd be this easy for them — without firing a shot." He turned away in deep and obvious contempt.

Melton came up out of the heat waves and danced a shimmering jig on the horizon. They rode steadily toward it, with only the slush-slush-slush of horses' hooves, the creak and grind of dry leather, and the musical sounds of rein chains and spur rowels to break the unnatural silence.

When Tom Elmore could see the tight clutch of people, Mexicans and three or four whites, up ahead, he startled Will with a roaring oath, wheeled his horse, drew his hand-gun in one smooth, swift gesture and shouted for his men to follow him. Some did.

They careened crazily across the open space toward a dense thicket of sage, and Will yelled out at them. But the shout was lost in a smashing fusillade of gunfire from the gunmen, that was directed into the thicket.

Stunned, Will cried out to the balance of the men to stay where they were. Some needed no urging. Like Will, they were flabbergasted at what was happening.

The thin wails of the townsmen came softly into the abrupt bedlam; then, as if they sprang out of the earth itself, a thin line of Indians appeared. There was a staggered flash of gunfire and after that the plain north of Melton became a crazy-quilt of cries, curses, flashing, vivid colors, men and animals.

Will dug in his spurs and thundered down the line of petrified gunmen, shouting for them to ride hard for the protection of the town. Only a few needed any urging.

Will heard the men around him shouting words that had no meaning. His horse grunted under repeated spurrings as he closed in behind the last rider and raced for Melton. Even if he had wanted to, there would have been no point in trying to help the fools who had followed Tom Elmore into the fight.

Riding with his head twisted backwards, he could see vague shapes of Apaches and gunmen flitting through the pall of heavy desert dust. Some mounted, more afoot, the Apaches tried to shoot the men's horses from under them first, then, at leisure, finish off the men.

Tom Elmore could not be identified. One gunman looked like another. The dust had a way of neutralizing all shapes and shirt colors. What brought his head back around was a roll of gunfire from the village. Up ahead, Matthews' gunmen had dismounted on the fly, their horses scurrying on down the crooked roadway, heads and tails high, and the gunmen themselves were forming a defensive line across the north end of the village, with their carbines flashing.

Will saw Matthews clearly enough to observe that he was scarlet-faced from throat to forehead, screaming orders with a big ivory-butted six-gun in his right fist. It angered him to see what Matthews was doing. He reined far wide of the gunmen and swerved in behind them. Almost before Matthews saw him, Will's handgun was making a vicious arc. Matthews opened his mouth to shout and threw up a defensive arm at the same time. Neither action saved him. The long gun barrel came down with a crushingly fierce slash, dashed aside the upflung arm and crunched solidly against the renegade leader's skull. The sound was lost in the tumult, but Will felt the impact all the way to his shoulder. Matthews went down like a dead man. He didn't roll once.

A gun went off close and the finger of death plucked lightly at Will's back. Without stopping his pistol's upward swing, he snapped off a shot. A fleeting glance had been enough. The tall, bony gunman Tom Elmore had once addressed as "George" collapsed with Will's slug deep in his chest.

Behind him somewhere a shotgun went off with an unmistakable roar. He winced and flung out of the saddle, lit in a low crouch and saw Grady Stewart holding the terrible weapon with black powdersmoke curling up from one barrel.

"Stop it, damn you! Stop that shootin'."

Flanked, demoralized by the things they had seen, the gunmen stared bewilderedly into Grady's shotgun and Will's cocked .45. They stopped firing.

The fight hadn't lasted five minutes. The firing died down and was replaced by a deathly stillness that was far worse than the noise had been. Someone grabbed Will from behind and tugged him around. It was Karen. Her face was flushed and her eyes were almost black with fright. "Stop it!" She repeated it five times in rapid succession. "Stop it! Stop it!"

He reached down, took one of her hands and shook her. "Quiet, Karen. Get hold of yourself."

The silence then became complete. He still held her hand when he faced back toward Matthews' gunmen.

"Put your guns down, boys. No — not in your holsters — on the ground." There was disbelief in every face. "I mean it. Put them on the ground."

They obeyed in a reluctant stupor, some shaking their heads as though the effort of thought and reason were too much right then.

"Grady, gather 'em up."

Grady walked up beside Will and looked with a sweating frown into his face. "What'll I do with this?" He held up the shotgun.

Will reached over and took the gun, passed it to Karen and jutted his chin toward the guns in the dust. Grady went forward, sweat dripping off his chin in a steady stream. A long way out, an Apache let off a high wailing scream. It arose to the highest pitch of the warrior's range, then broke off into a series of little coyote barks and ended with the coughing snarl of a cougar. Coldly, Will thought it was a very appropriate finale to the skirmish.

When Grady had the gunmen disarmed Will turned toward the Mexicans who were coming back out of hiding, clutching ancient rifles and Indian bows and arrows. He singled out one tall, youthful-looking Mexican and spoke to him in staccato Spanish.

"Build a fire, *compadre*. Make it no larger than your sombrero and right there — in the middle of the road."

The Mexican looked surprised but went to work gathering little faggots. Everyone watched him in fascination except Will. He was looking out where the fight had taken place. There were bodies out there. He tried to count them, got as high as seven, then heard someone calling for water.

"Grady, dump the guns here. Good. Take four or five Mexicans and go get that man that's hollering out there."

The Mexicans shrank back from the undertaking in spite of Grady's exhortations. He finally took two of the disarmed gunmen and trudged scowlingly, eyes slitted and wary, out where the dead men were. Of eleven, Mike Allen was the only one left alive. They brought him back and took him into the trading post and made him as comfortable as they could on a smelly pile of Navaho blankets.

In the meantime the little fire was burning lustily. Will holstered his gun and spoke to Karen without looking away from the bleary-eyed, dusty and sweat-streaked gunmen.

"Was there ever a jail in Melton?"

"No, but my father used to use a little dungeon room under the old barn for his *vaqueros* when they needed sobering up."

"Will it hold these men?"

"Oh, yes. It might be a little crowded, but they won't be able to get out. There's only the trap door, and it's reinforced with steel."

"Does Grady know where it is?"

"I doubt it. It hasn't been used since long before my father died."

Will beckoned the trader over. "Grady, Karen's going to show you where Maxwell's old *calabozo* is under the barn. Take these men down there and lock them in it. Put five or six Mexicans over them as guards and give the Mexicans all the guns they want."

Grady flicked sweat off his forehead. "All right. Didn't know there was such a place." He pointed at the sprawled figure. "How about the judge there? Him too?"

"Yes, take Matthews with you. He's no judge; unless I miss my guess he's an outlaw of the first water. Toss him in there, too."

Karen was looking at the unconscious man. "Will, his head's bleeding!"

Will studied the blood-matted hair then lowered his glance to Matthews' chest. The respiration was even and deep. He had only a superficial wound despite his gory appearance. "He'll be all right." He nodded at the apathetic-looking

187

gunmen. "Have a couple of them hoist him up, Grady. Take as many Mexicans as you want and make sure these men'll stay down in that hole, before you put 'em in there."

Grady barked orders. The gunmen began to move out in a shuffling line. They were beaten and they knew it.

Will swung across the trailing line of listless men and watched them for a moment; then he went over to the little fire and knelt by it, took off his hat, held it above the flames to test the wind-drift. He scooped up a handful of dust and threw it over the blaze, keeping his hat over the rising smudge until the smoke was billowing around it, then jerked it swiftly upwards. A fat little puff of dirty-looking smoke mushroomed straight up. He turned when a shadow fell across the fire. It was Karen. He shook off the sweat on his face and spoke.

"Green brush'd be better, but dust'll do. Anyway, they're close enough to see us without the signal fire."

"Who's close enough, Will?"

"Juan Soldado's Apaches."

He looked back to the fire and made two more passes over the smoke, sending up the call for Juan Soldado to come closer and show himself in plain sight. Will missed the quick spasm of fear that passed over Karen's face.

Finished, he straightened up and kicked enough dust over the fire to smother it. The sun was burning into his skull. He blew into his hat

188

and put it back on. The tangy smell of smoke clung to him. He reached down and caught Karen's fingers in his fist, looked around at the watching Mexicans and the few white renegades who were like statues. He smiled thinly at the men who hadn't ridden out with Tom Elmore's crew and spoke first in English, then in Spanish.

"Don't a one of you touch a gun. The Apaches have Melton surrounded and outnumber you ten to one. They are coming into town and they are coming peaceably, but the first fool who touches a gun will get every man and woman here killed, including himself."

The Mexicans nodded. He singled out the remnants of Matthews' gang and saw a defiant uncertainty in their faces.

"You boys that came in with Matthews — or Curtin, if you knew him by that name — don't try to ride away. The Apaches are waiting out there for you to try and cross the desert. They'll kill every one of you who tries it. If you're smart you'll shed those guns and act like you love Apaches, because I don't think the Indians 're going to like the looks of white men wearing guns, after what Elmore tried to do."

He turned away and, still clutching Karen's hand, walked back to the northern extremity of Melton and stopped wide-legged, in plain view, beyond the last house. He could feel the quiver that passed through Karen. Standing there looking out where the dead men still lay with their horses under the brassy sun, he waited as he'd done earlier that morning. Once, Karen tightened her fingers around his fist.

"What are we waiting for, Will?"

"Juan Soldado."

Her quick silence made him more than ever conscious of the inherent fear she had of Apaches. He understood it; it was endemic on the frontier.

"Guillermo!"

Will looked toward the sound. He recognized the thin, astringent face, the strong, scarred body and the defiant stance of the Apache leader. Juan Soldado was standing beyond the farthest dead gunman, legs spread and his carbine clutched in both hands. Behind him were four more Apaches, identical in appearance except for the fact that their leader was older.

"Juan."

The Indian spoke to his companions, then started forward afoot. Will closed his fingers around Karen's hand and drew her with him. They walked together. Her palm was suddenly hot and damp. Will said nothing. When they were close enough Juan Soldado stopped and let his black, beady gaze linger on Karen's face. In Spanish he said, "She's scared, Guillermo." There was a flicker of dark amusement in the Indian's eyes.

Will nodded. "It is the same with your women, Juan."

"Yes," he answered; then, "Why did that fool charge the brush, Guillermo?"

"I don't know. I made him wait back there until I was sure you saw me; then I brought them back here. I think he felt that he had to, because he'd told his leader he would catch some Apaches alive."

"Ah! He was more foolish than he acted, then." The black eyes switched to Karen again. It was as though Juan Soldado had dismissed the fight as being trivial. "She'll make you a good woman, Guillermo. Deep-bellied women are the best. Like horses, they last a long time."

Will could feel the color beating under his skin. So long as they spoke in Spanish, though, he felt safe enough. "She is the daughter of a man named Maxwell who used to ranch in this country."

"Yes," Juan Soldado said with a quick, bird-like nod that was both understanding and approving, "I know who she is. When she was very little her father used to bring her to visit us. She was a baby then. It was a long time ago." The Apache's black eyes jumped back to Will's face. "I have a wounded warrior, Guillermo. One of those fools got him in the hip with a wild shot."

"Let's go to him."

Juan shook his head. "No, they are bringing him up here. We'll wait."

While they waited the Apache leader asked Will what else was to be done. Will could feel Karen's grip relaxing a little. He gave her fingers a quick, hard squeeze before he answered.

"Keep your surround, Juan, until the posse from Tucson gets here. After that . . ."

"It won't be long. Didn't you see the signal from the ramparts above the rancheria?"

"No."

Juan shook his head in mock disapproval. "When you were out on the desert; that's what my first signal fire was about, telling the warriors down here that we must be very careful. I thought maybe you were riding to meet this other band of white men." He shrugged in a typically Mexican way. "The posse is close. It should be here by early afternoon."

Four Apache fighting men came lurching out of the brush with a burden that was a fifth warrior lying in an improvised stretcher made of strong-smelling saddle blankets. Without a word they carried the injured man up to Will's feet and laid him down, then grouped their bodies so as to provide shade and watched intently as Will bent, probed the wound, wiped away the blood and went grimly to work with his pocketknife, digging for the bullet.

The Apache never once made a sound, but Karen turned away and Juan Soldado's mouth was tugged flat over his teeth and his black eyes shone appraisingly as Will finally located the piece of lead and began to work it out of the badly swollen, purplish flesh. Sweat dripped steadily from his face as he worked. He grunted when at last the pellet popped out and fell onto the dirty blanket. He picked it up, gazed at it, held it out and smiled when the wounded man reached for it. Bandaging was simple and primitive. When it was all over Will stood up and let out his breath.

"Juan, send him back to the fishing spot. Have him stay there in the shade near the water and wash his wound twice a day. Will he do that?"

"To save his life — yes." Juan told the man what to do in a casual, off-hand way, then turned his back upon him. He stared at the men who were behind him. The warrior trotted away instantly, and Juan spread his hands, palms upward. "He is a poor man, that warrior. He has no horses, hardly, but he will pay you. In the meantime I sent for the little white boys. That'll keep you pleased maybe, until you can be better paid."

"I don't want any pay. I'll never take pay from your people."

"You are the only good white man I have ever known, Guillermo."

Will brushed aside the compliment with embarrassment. "I'd forgotten the boys. You have them here, too?"

"Of course. I knew it must be so. Send your squaw to the village with them. They need white man's food, maybe."

Karen spoke for the first time, in Spanish as fluent as Will's had been. "The Thorndike boys, Will?"

It shocked him so that he blinked at her. "Yes. Karen, I didn't think you understood."

"I was raised among the Mexicans, you know."

He blushed scarlet, remembering Juan Soldado's personal observations. When the boys came, he handed them over to her and watched her lead them back toward the village and up the dusty roadway toward the trading post. It was Juan Soldado's chuckle that brought his attention back to the Indian.

"I knew, Guillermo. I thought you knew too."

Will avoided re-opening the subject by sidestepping it altogether. "Call in your warriors, Juan. We'll all go into Melton and wait for the men from Tucson."

Juan hesitated. Once, thirty years before, he had been in Melton. That was when old Maxwell had ruled the country. Much had happened since then. Like all Apaches, he considered Mexicans to be the most treacherous people on earth, and Juan Soldado, like every other Apache leader from Mangas to Geronimo, had reason to believe this.

Sensing Juan's apprehension, Will explained what had happened since the fight with Matthews' renegades. The Indian listened stoically, his eyes gazing toward the village hot and pensive. After a long moment he shrugged and spoke.

"Let's go."

Will waited until he had called up a spindly-legged, massive-torsoed warrior and growled in guttural Apache to him; then they went toward the village.

The silence was heavy and brooding. There was tension in the air. When they were close enough to see the men standing in the shade watching them approach, Juan Soldado picked out the Americans with his darting eyes and spoke in an aside to Will.

"You didn't put them all away, Guillermo."

"There was no need. Those are harmless. If you wish I'll have them locked up too."

Reassured but wary, the Apache grunted and said no more.

The Mexicans watched the Apache warriors filter into their village from the desert with wet, flashing eyes. They were like people carved from some dark wood, so motionless, so tense and fearful were they.

Will waited until the roadway was filled with the warriors. He and Juan Soldado stood side by side under the ramada of Grady's trading post. "Tell them they are safe, Juan," he said. "There must be no trouble."

Juan Soldado spoke to the men. He harangued them with his not inconsiderable oratorical ability, but all the time he spoke his black eyes were roaming restlessly over the white men, and when he finished telling his warriors there must be no fighting under any circumstances, he turned swiftly and touched Will's chest with his fingers.

"You talk to your people now, Guillermo."

Will did. He reiterated what he had said before. Then, further to ease the tension, he detailed eleven Mexicans, under the young man who had built the signal fire in the roadway, to go out and haul away the dead horses and fetch back the dead gunmen. As a final suggestion, he called upon the Mexicans to bring out food for the Apaches.

It worked. Inactivity heightened tension more readily than movement did. The Apaches stayed a little apart, squatting in the shade, impassive, alert with an animal wariness, until the beans and tortillas and other foods were brought out and presented to them. The ice thawed quickly enough. Both the Indians and the Mexicans had a common ground in the Spanish language. The village became more animated. There was even laughter and a little banter. Only Matthews' few remaining gunmen stayed apart. Seeing this, Will turned to Juan under the shade of the ramada.

"I'm going to have those outlaws penned up, Juan. You stay out here and watch your people until I get back."

"Good. I like what I see now. There will be no trouble."

Will entered the trading post and immediately saw the Thorndike boys, burnt as dark as any Apache children, squatting near the curtained off doorway, sipping lemonade. He also saw something else. Karen and a feverish-faced Grady Stewart were loitering over the pile of Indian blankets where Mike Allen lay, bleeding to death internally. Until that moment he had forgotten the wounded man.

"Grady?"

The trader lifted his head and swung it, waiting. There was anger in his eyes.

"Will you take the remainder of Curtin's gunmen and lock them up, too? The Mexicans won't start any trouble and I'm sure Juan Soldado's Apaches won't, but I don't like the looks of those killers. Even without their guns I don't like the looks of them."

"Sure," Grady said in a dull way. "Glad to." He looked back down at Mike Allen. "Be back directly." Then he went out.

Will walked over beside Karen and was shocked at the pale grey look of the fat man. Allen tried to smile at him. It was a dismal failure. "Going out," he said huskily. "Won't be long. Trying to clear up a few things beforehand, Graham."

"Don't talk," Karen said.

Will saw the wound; a slanting shot through both lungs. It wouldn't be long. His trained mind told him that. Mike Allen spoke again.

"Matthews killed a man in Tucson, a man Judge Curtin was sending over here to find his nephews. He hired those gunmen from his saloons and came over himself. It was gold. . . ."

"I know," Will said. "But you're no gunman. How'd you come to get mixed up in it?"

"He had me over a barrel. There was some trouble. I was a dealer at one of his house games. Poker. He bought me out of it — used that over my head and made me come along."

"All right," Will said. "Don't talk any more."
Then he bent and probed the wound. Karen
watched him with an intent look.

Chapter 9

Juan Soldado's estimate of the time when the posse from Tucson would arrive proved correct. When a bushy-headed, heavy-paunched man with the two big guns girded around his ample middle and hard blue eyes reined up outside the trading post and swung down and stomped off the dust with a deep scowl, Will was standing under the ramada with Karen and Grady and Juan Soldado, watching.

Juan's estimate of the number of hard-bitten men from Tucson who had accompanied the judge across the scorching desert was also accurate.

"I'm Judge Curtin. Is there a man around here named Will Graham?"

Will stepped forward and introduced himself. He then introduced the others and, lastly, Juan Soldado. The judge looked long and hard at the Apache, who returned the look. Then Curtin blew out a big gust of breath through his nose and stepped under the ramada with a gesture toward his men and horses. "Mister Stewart, sir."

Grady understood and nodded, moving out into the smashing heat and beckoning the possemen down toward the old barn.

"Mister Graham. . . ."

"Just plain Will, Judge."

"Good. I like that. Will, tell me everything you know about this business."

Will did. While he was talking Karen slipped inside for the lemonade all desert wayfarers put such store by. When Will had finished his recital, Judge Curtin threw Karen a deep old-fashioned bow and accepted his lemonade. He turned and gazed at Juan Soldado, who was torn between a desire to emulate the white men with glasses in their hands and a natural aversion to the tangy odor of lemonade.

"Juan Soldado," the judge said in a booming voice, "I never thought I'd offer my hand to an Apache — but here it is."

Juan, to Will's surprise, looked downright embarrassed. He took the judge's huge paw, pumped it once and dropped it very quickly.

Karen brought the Thorndike boys out. With squeals they ran to Judge Curtin and threw their skinny arms around his massive legs and gulped fiercely to hide the hot-burning tears that scalded their eyes and ran down their cheeks.

The judge dropped down heavily on one knee and engulfed the boys in his arms. Will turned self-consciously away. Curtin's heavily armed, granite-faced and deeply sunburnt riders were walking back up toward the trading post. They eyed the Apache warriors with askance glances. Grady Stewart stepped into the shade, shot a quick look at the lads and their uncle and looked just as swiftly away. He sighed gustily and shook his head to fling off the perspiration.

"Is it all over, Will? It's hard to believe."

"This part of it is," Will said. "The Apache wars aren't."

Grady nodded in silence and watched Karen urging more lemonade on Juan Soldado. The Indian's glistening face was wreathed in a tentative, doubting smile. Karen re-filled the glass anyway, then went into the trading post to get more of the juice. Grady followed her in.

Judge Curtin stood up with two small hands clutched in his big fists. "Will, golly, I don't know what to say — what to offer you."

"Nothing," Will said quietly. "If you'd do as much for me — for my kids — I'd say we're even."

The judge studied Will's face for a long moment of silence, broken only by the sounds of spurs as his possemen from Tucson walked in under the ramada's overhang; then he nodded his head.

"I'd do as much, Will, for your kids or anyone's kids. Any man would, I reckon."

"There's something you can do for the man who's really responsible for your nephews being alive, Judge."

"Name it. Name the man, too."

"Juan Soldado. You can be influential in getting his rancheria made into a reservation for his band."

"Influential!" the judge boomed. "By golly,

201

Will, I'm the boundary commissioner in this part of the Territory for In'jun reservations. I can order his rancheria set aside permanently for his band."

Will looked at the Apache and told him in Spanish what Judge Curtin had said. Juan's black eyes held on Will's face. He didn't thank the judge. He thanked Will.

"A man's heart tells him when he has found his brother, Guillermo. I knew it was thus when we first met. You are my brother. You are my people's father. Tell this big-bellied man he must also make you our White Father; then I swear to you, no man of Juan Soldado's band will ever take up the knife against the white people again. Tell him that, Guillermo — I want to hear him answer it."

Judge Curtin did better than answer it. He turned and spoke in perfect Spanish, looking straight at Juan Soldado, man to man. The Apache grunted, then swiftly walked away from them all with his face held perfectly rigid. But Will saw the look in his eyes. It was enough.

"Are any of these men lawmen, Judge?"

Curtin smiled flintily and nodded toward a hawkish-looking man with level eyes. "This here's the United States marshal. That good enough?"

"Yes." Will turned. "Would you like to see the prisoners?"

"Already have," the marshal said in a clipped way. "Saw 'em when we were puttin' up our horses."

"Well," Will said, a little at a loss, "I reckon it's all out of my hands then, isn't it?"

He left them shortly after that, a feeling of loneliness engulfing him suddenly. He went down to the barn, saw that his horse had been cared for, walked away from the loafing men down there and sought the shade of the barn's rear wall. The adobe was cool. He smoked and stared out toward the Galiuros. Instinctively, he thought of the fishing hole. He'd go up there for a few weeks and rest.

"Will?"

He saw her stepping hesitantly around the rear doorway of the old barn her father had built. There was a hint of a frown puckering the soft flesh between her eyes. He smashed out the cigarette and answered:

"Here."

"Oh, I didn't see you. Come on up to the post. We're all going to eat together." She came over beside him. "The judge wants it that way." Then, as though remembering something, she said, "I think he's wonderful, don't you?"

"Yes. At least he's better'n the last Judge Curtin we had here."

"Will?"

He sensed a difference in her tone. "Yes?"

She didn't look directly at him now, but a little past his face. "Grady followed me into the trading post when I went after more lemonade."

"I know — I saw him."

"Will, he asked me if you'd buy the post. He

asked me if I thought you would."

"What did you tell him?" The idea had never occurred to Will. In fact it startled him now, as he turned it over in his mind.

"I said you probably wouldn't, because you're a doctor, not a trader."

"You're observant, aren't you?"

"It's all I wanted to know, Will," she said in a quick rush of words. "I didn't really care. You could have been an outlaw like Mike Allen thought you were. But I wanted to know."

"I was a medical man in Santa Fe, Karen. My wife ran off with an old friend of mine. That's all the mystery there is to me."

"And you loved her, Will. I know that."

"Yes, of course. We'd been married four years. I loved her all right." He looked away from her. "That's all done with now though, Karen. All behind me."

She opened her mouth to speak, then closed it tightly, waited a second and opened it again. "But what would you want with a trading post?"

He looked over at her in a droll way. "You're good at fishing for information, honey, but as a schemer you're a dismal failure."

"What do you mean, Will?"

"You want me to buy Grady's trading post."

"No, not exactly. I . . ."

"I'll tell you the terms on which I'll buy it then. If you'll marry me. I just thought of the most beautiful spot in Arizona for a honeymoon — up in Juan Soldado's country by a fishing hole. We could go up there. I'd teach you to fish. There are the fattest trout up there you ever saw, Karen."

She looked as if she were going to laugh or cry, he didn't know which, before she spoke again. "I'm not sure I want to compete with a fat trout." She flushed a dark red and looked down at her feet. "You see, I own just about all the country around Melton. It was our old ranch. If we owned the trading post, the ranch, and you were Indian agent, we'd prosper, Will."

"But you haven't said you loved me."

Her eyes flashed at him. "You're supposed to do that — not me."

"All right. I love you, Karen. I guess I have for a long time. You're Arizona to me."

"I'd rather just be a woman — to you."

"Arizona's a woman: a beautiful, unchanging, very strong woman. I love her very much. It's taken time for her to grow on me, Karen, like it has for you to grow on me, but I'll never be happy anywhere else or with anyone else. You belong here, to this country."

"So do you, Will. I've always thought that. You belong to me and to Arizona, and I love you."

He felt a little weak inside. The cool old adobe wall at his back was a welcome support. "I reckon this Judge Curtin from Tucson could marry us, couldn't he?"

"Yes."

He turned and looked at her. It was a frightening moment for both of them. "Tonight," he said, "in the little church where we've sat and talked."

"Yes."

He saw the tears coming then and felt an odd thickness in his own throat as he reached for her, brought her close against him and held her like that until someone, a long way off, began beating insistently on an iron wagon tire suspended from a tree limb, calling them to supper.